THE HOUSE OF MIRRORS

THE HOUSE OF MIRRORS

SCHOLASTIC INC.
New York Toronto London Auckland Sydney
Mexico City New Delhi Hong Kong Buenos Aires

No part of this publication may be reproduced, stored in a retrieval system, or transmitted in any form or by any means, electronic, mechanical, photocopying, recording, or otherwise, without written permission of the publisher. For information regarding permission, write to Scholastic Inc., Attention: Permissions Department, 557 Broadway, New York, NY 10012.

ISBN 13: 978-0-439-77672-1
ISBN 10: 0-439-77672-4

Copyright © 2005 by Edizioni Piemme S.p.A., via del Carmine 5, 15033 Casale Monferrato (AL), Italia.
English translation © 2007 by Edizioni Piemme S.p.A.

Text by Pierdomenico Baccalario
Original title: La Casa Degli Specchi
Graphics by Iacopo Bruno and Laura Zuccotti
Original cover and illustrations by Iacopo Bruno
Editorial project by Marcella Drago and Clare Stringer

Special thanks to James Preller
Special thanks to Lidia Morson Tramontozzi
Design by Timothy Hall

12 11 10 9 8 7 6 5 4 3 2   8 9 10 11 12/0

Printed in the U.S.A.
First printing, September 2007

Dear Reader,

As soon as our editor, Michael Merryweather, sent us the third manuscript written by the mysterious Ulysses Moore, we rushed to publish it as soon as possible. You have no idea how impatiently we wait for his e-mails. Each time he writes, we scan through the pages, hoping to find out something new about this baffling town and its mysterious people.

Like us, you'll notice that in this book there's no shortage of surprises!

Your friends at
Scholastic

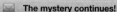

From: Michael Merryweather
Date: July 14, 2006 1:56 PM
To: The editors at Scholastic Inc.
Subject: The mystery continues!
Attachment: Copy of Guide to Kilmore Cove

Here's the translation of Ulysses Moore's third journal. What I have discovered is utterly incredible. But before you start reading the journal, I must tell you what happened last week. I was told there's a tourist bookstore in Ermington, a town not far from my bed-and-breakfast. I rushed there hoping to learn more about Kilmore Cove.

I searched through the books, manuscripts, notebooks, maps and charts, legends, and stories on Cornwall without finding anything. I found nothing, nada, zip on Kilmore Cove. It's almost as if the town does not exist!

Disgusted that I failed to find even the smallest clue, I went to an outdoor café for a cup of coffee. At first, I didn't notice a distinguished-looking gentleman sitting at the table next to me, and now, no matter how hard I try to picture him, I only remember a huge mustache and a white linen shirt. When I finished, I went inside to pay. When I came out, I found this book on my table:

The Curious Traveler
A Mini-Guide to Kilmore Cove and Its Surroundings

Trembling, I opened the little book. On the first page, in a handwriting that I know well, he had written:

FROM THE MOORES' PRIVATE COLLECTION
Argo Manor, Kilmore Cove

Only then did I realize that the man sitting near my table was gone. Inside the book there was a photo of the old train station in Kilmore Cove. This book is proof that Kilmore Cove exists! And that it's here, nearby! I give you my word that I will find it, even if I have to comb Cornwall in its entirety . . . I'll write you as soon as I can.

MM

Contents

V. MARBEUF.
Fabricant d'instruments d'Optique et de Mathématiques
Rue Royale, 70, a Brest.

THE HOUSE OF MIRRORS

- Chapter 1 -
BREAKFAST

BIRD ALLEY

K

WHALES CALF

SHARP HEELS

A tourist's map
of the little town
KILMORE COVE
in Cornwall

Julia awoke to the smell of bacon. She rolled over in bed, pulled the warm blankets around her shoulders, and burrowed her head into the pillow. She felt warm, relaxed, like she could lie in bed forever.

But then suddenly, everything that had happened yesterday came flooding back to her. The storm, the terror, the man who had chased after her trying to steal the key — falling, falling over the cliff.

Julia shook her head, heart pounding. She looked around. Safe. Home. She was in Kilmore Cove, in Argo Manor, in her bedroom. At the bottom of the bed there was a pile of wet clothes. It was real, not a dream.

Julia leaped out of bed. "Jason!" she cried.

Julia picked her clothes up from the floor and searched the pocket of her pants. Yes, they were still there — the four keys to the Door to Time.

What time was it? Light was leaking through the window blinds. Was it morning or afternoon?

Still in her pajamas, Julia wandered into the hallway. "Jason? Rick?" Had they made it back? She couldn't remember. It was all a fog, a feverish dream.

Julia pushed open the door to Jason's bedroom. It was dark, and the curtains were pulled across the window. The bed was unmade. Julia saw two pairs of sneakers on the floor, some crumpled T-shirts piled on the dresser. *A mess*, she thought with a smile. Jason's mess.

Suddenly she heard her twin brother's voice from downstairs. He was okay. He was back. He was safe!

Julia turned and bounded down the stairs in threes. She raced into the kitchen.

Jason and Rick were standing close together at the stove. Jason was stirring a pan of scrambled eggs.

Julia rushed into their arms. Rick seemed only too glad to enjoy Julia's warm embrace, but Jason downplayed the peril. "Of course we came back," Jason said with a shrug. "Don't get all mushy on me. Everything's fine."

Ignoring her brother (Julia was well-practiced in the art), she stepped back to take a good look at the two adventurers. To her disappointment, they looked exactly the same. If their experience on the other side of the door had changed them at all, their outward appearance gave no sign.

"How are you guys?" she asked.

"Hungry," Jason said.

"Starving," Rick added.

They greedily filled three plates with eggs, toast, and bacon. The sky outside was clear and bright, so they ate out on the patio.

Watching the boys eat, stuffing their faces like

dogs, Julia couldn't stand it any longer. "Are you going to tell me or what?" she demanded.

Rick set down his fork. He looked Julia in the eyes. "It's almost too much to explain," he said. "Like this bizarre dream world — but it was real, Julia. Everything was real."

Jason glanced at Julia, nodded, and continued eating.

"I was so worried about you . . ." Julia began. And then she felt it — not tears, but moisture in her eyes. Angry at herself, Julia looked toward the garden, blinking the wetness away. She had held it together all day yesterday. The waiting, the worrying, the attack, and the terrible storm. Through it all, Julia had been strong and brave. But now, sitting here in the garden watching her brother stuff himself with bacon, she felt herself begin to crumble.

"We were worried about you, too," Rick said.

Jason smiled at his sister. "I knew you'd be okay, Julia. I just felt it in my bones."

Julia liked that, and she understood it. No matter how they fought, no matter what happened between them, Julia and Jason were connected — as if an invisible cord bound them together. Twins. Brother and sister. A matched set.

"It was amazing, Julia," Rick told her. And with

that, the two boys told their tale. Rick would begin a sentence, and Jason would interrupt to finish it. All the while Julia sat in rapt attention. Amazed, stunned, relieved; she believed every word, and every word was true.

The past twenty-four hours had been amazing. Julia and Jason and their parents had just moved to Argo Manor, an ancient manor in Kilmore Cove, on the coast of Cornwall. With their new friend Rick, the twins had set out to explore the old house. And they'd discovered something beyond their wildest flights of imagination — a strange old door that had led to a great sailing ship called the *Metis*, hidden in an enormous grotto. After a strange storm of sorts, the ship had brought the kids to the other side of the grotto — and to ancient Egypt. It was there that they had accidentally become separated, with Julia returning to Argo Manor while the boys tried desperately to figure out what had happened to them.

Their quest had led them to Maruk, a young Egyptian girl who had taken them on a tour through the House of Life, an ancient storing place for all sorts of information. There Rick and Jason had picked up the trail of clues left by the elusive Ulysses Moore, the former owner of Argo Manor.

It seemed Ulysses Moore had concealed a map of Kilmore Cove in the House of Life for safekeeping — and had moved it again when its security was threatened. It had taken all of Rick, Jason, and Maruk's ingenuity, but they had located the map — only to have it stolen away from them by Oblivia Newton, a treacherous woman who seemed determined to uncover all of Ulysses Moore's secrets.

"We'll find that map, we'll get it back," Jason concluded fiercely.

Rick nodded in agreement. Their minds were made up. The map was the key — and they were determined to reclaim it, one way or the other.

Julia took it all in, never interrupting, just listening. She felt all quivery and uncertain.

When Julia reached for a glass of juice, Rick noticed that her hands were shaking. "What's wrong?" Rick asked. "Are you frightened?"

Julia shook her head. "No, it's just — it's just that I'm so happy to see you. There were times, last night, when I wasn't so sure if I ever would again."

For the first time the boys, absorbed in their own heroic deeds, seemed to notice Julia. She was part of the team, too, even though she had not shared their journey to the Land of Punt.

Jason glanced around the yard as if seeing it for the first time. Tree limbs were down, flowers were beaten by the wind and rain, old bushes looked damaged. "It looks like you guys got hit by a tornado," he gasped.

In the middle of the main flower bed, Jason saw tire tracks. He looked at his sister. "Hey," he said with concern. "Julia, what happened here?"

Julia felt her heartbeat accelerate again, faster and faster. Her head swam as she relived the terrors of the previous night. She looked toward the edge of the cliff and listened for the churning sea below.

She closed her eyes. And she remembered.

"What's the matter, Julia?" Rick asked. She had turned ghostly pale. "Are you all right?"

"It wasn't my fault," Julia said, her eyes wide with horror. "He came at me . . . I had no choice . . . and he jumped . . . and he flew . . . flew into emptiness . . . and then . . . and then . . . he was gone."

Talking slowly, her voice void of expression, Julia told them everything that had transpired at Argo Manor the previous night. She told them of how Nestor confessed that the previous owner, Ulysses Moore, did indeed take many trips aboard the *Metis*. She related how Manfred had tried to get into the house, and how she and Nestor had fought him, resisted him, until the tragic end.

"I think it served him right," Jason remarked coldly. "He got what he deserved."

Julia looked at her brother with a mixture of surprise and horror. "But Jason," she protested. "No one deserves . . ."

"He was a thief!" Jason spat angrily. "A thief just like his boss, Oblivia Newton. They have no right," he muttered, fists clenched. "No right."

To change the mood, Rick began recalling more of the previous day's incredible journey. He described the House of Life in exquisite detail, and spoke of Maruk, the Pharaoh, and the strange woman who worked in Maruk's father's office. Soon the boys were laughing, describing how they had dangled from the statue of Osiris. "And those snakes!" Jason shouted gleefully, laughing. "Tell her about the snakes!"

"One dropped on my head!" Rick exclaimed. At this, both boys guffawed, clutching their stomachs, sides splitting with laughter.

But their merriment quickly faded when they thought of what happened next — Oblivia had stolen the map from right under their noses.

"I still can't believe she was there," Julia said, shaking her head in shock. "How is that possible?"

"How is anything possible?" Rick replied.

"Everything is possible," Jason joined in. "If we've learned anything since coming to Argo Manor, it's that there is no such thing as impossible."

"This morning, Jason came up with a new theory," Rick explained to Julia, who was struggling to comprehend everything they'd told her. "Jason isn't completely convinced that we traveled through time."

"Okaaay," Julia said doubtfully. "But it's not like you took a bus."

Jason offered, "I read a book by an expert in this stuff and he mentioned something similar. It's not called 'time traveling.'"

Julia glanced at Rick, raising her eyebrows. "What do they call it, then? Jumping down the rabbit hole like Alice in Wonderland?"

Jason ignored her. "It's called something-something . . . space-time continuum . . . whatchamacallit . . ."

"Oh, that's catchy!" Julia said with mock enthusiasm.

"It's not a joke," Jason insisted. "I was there, Julia. I felt it. And I'm telling you, I just didn't feel like I was in a time or space completely different than ours."

He paused, then whispered, "It almost felt like home."

"Right," Julia said, "except it was sandier and filled with Houses of the Dead and snakes and stuff like that."

"But check this out, Julia," Rick said with seriousness. "We could speak the same language as those

people, and we could read hieroglyphics as if we were reading a billboard on the side of the road."

Julia stared at him in disbelief.

Rick reached into his trusty backpack and produced the *Dictionary of Forgotten Languages*. He opened it to the page for languages of ancient Egypt and put his finger under some hieroglyphics. "Sitting here, in this yard, I can't read a word of this, Julia. I have no idea what it says."

Jason nodded. "But back there, down that rabbit hole or whatever you want to call it, we could read every word."

"Tell me more about Oblivia," Julia said.

"We were hiding," Rick said. "We heard her talking. She mentioned Ulysses Moore."

"What?" asked Julia in disbelief.

"And she was looking for the map," Rick said. "She was desperate to find it."

"But we found it first," Jason said with a hint of triumph.

"Yeah, but she took it from us," Rick said.

"Stole it," Jason corrected.

Julia held up her hands. "Slow down, rewind," she said. "What was it a map of?"

Rick recited the words from memory: "The first and only accurate map of that land in Cornwall known as Kilmore Cove."

A loud, violent sneeze interrupted their conversation. It was the caretaker, Nestor, emerging from his cottage. He came up the steep steps slowly, stopping once in a while to catch his breath. To Rick, he looked like an old, tired man.

"I see you've eaten," Nestor said approvingly. Once again he sneezed, three times, in short blasts, then dabbed his nose with what looked like a dirty rag.

"You've caught yourself a nasty cold, haven't you?" noted Jason.

"The rain," murmured Nestor, by way of explanation. He looked at Julia with a furtive smile. "How are you feeling, child?"

"Oh, I'm fine," Julia answered. "Just another boring day. Oh, sure, Jason and Rick have been telling me all about their adventures in Egypt . . . with the child Pharaoh! But other than that, everything's same-o, same-o, just the regular stuff."

Rick smiled. He enjoyed Julia's deadpan humor. She had a certain something to her, some zip, or wit. Whatever it was, he liked it.

"Oh yeah," Julia added, glaring at Nestor. "You'll never guess who else they ran into, out there in the space-time something-or-other."

Nestor's eyes narrowed. He shrugged. "Surprise me."

"Oblivia Newton," Julia answered.

Nestor's lips tightened; his gaze grew cold and distant. He reached for the back of a chair and eased himself into it. "Tell me," he said to the boys. "I must know everything."

As the story unfolded, Nester grew agitated. "I should have foreseen it," he remarked when the boys were finished. "That woman is more dangerous than I had thought. Clearly, she will stop at nothing."

"Why is the map so important?" asked Jason.

"I have no idea," grumbled the caretaker. He avoided Jason's skeptical gaze.

"Maybe you don't," Jason shot back, "but Ulysses knew. I believe that he sent us there to find it. But why, Nestor? There must be a good reason."

"We had it in our hands," Rick said in frustration.

"It doesn't matter," Jason replied angrily. "We don't have it anymore. That's the only thing that matters now. Not who got there first . . ."

". . . but who laughs last," Julia said.

"I want another chance at that map," Jason said. His determination was searing, a white-hot blaze of single-minded focus. "Ulysses Moore wants us to find that map!"

"How can you possibly know he's even alive?" Julia demanded.

"Wake up, Julia," Jason said, his voice flooded

with emotion. "Somebody keeps leaving us clues. It's like we're being guided along the way — like an unseen hand is pushing us along."

"Did you get knocked on the head when you were in Egypt?" Julia asked. "Because you are talking crazy-talk."

Jason frowned. "Think whatever you want, Julia. It's no sweat off my back. The only thing I care about now is finding that map." He turned to Nestor. "Got any ideas?"

Nestor nodded his head. "Ideas? Yes, I do, in fact. It's time for me to get to work. The grounds are a disaster. There is much to do and I have dawdled too long already." He rose to leave.

"Oh no you don't!" Jason said. "You have to start giving us some answers, starting right now."

"Oh really?" asked Nestor, amused. "And how will you stop me? Tie me up? Hit me with a shovel?" The caretaker stood up stiffly and massaged his neck with a rough hand.

"You've got to help us!" pleaded Jason. "Please, Nestor. He's still here, isn't he?"

Nestor chuckled. "Your head is filled with too many stories," he said dismissively.

"Then swear to it," Jason challenged. "Put your hand on a bible and swear to us that he's not here!"

The old man placed his hands on his hips and arched his back. His face looked more tired, more drained, than even yesterday — as if he had aged a year's time in one night. His eyes were glassy, like he was running a fever.

"You look sick," Julia said, breaking the standoff. "Are you all right, Nestor?"

"Never mind that," Jason insisted. "We must know the truth if we want to understand what's happening! There are too many things we don't know! We're in the middle of this now, Nestor, whether you like it or not."

Nestor looked at his small cottage in the garden, then back at the kids. Jason was right. They were groping in the dark, filled with fears and doubts. Perhaps it was getting too dangerous.

He sighed deeply, then he placed a hand on Jason's shoulder and spoke with earnest warmth. "Dear child, I swear upon my mother's grave that no Moore lives in Argo Manor. Are you happy now?"

Then he hobbled away, limping as much as ever, blowing his nose as he went.

Rick watched him go. "Technically," he whispered to his friends, "he didn't tell us that Ulysses was dead."

"Technically," Jason echoed, "he never tells us anything."

Once breakfast was over, Rick walked out to the edge of the cliff. He gazed at the sea, feeling the light breeze in his hair. Julia, who had gone back to her room to get properly dressed, returned with the four keys, each in the shape of an animal. She found Jason in the same chair he'd been sitting in when she left. He appeared lost in thought. A pen and paper lay in front of him on the table.

"I don't know where to begin," he confided.

Julia stood beside her brother, reading over his shoulder. "Do we know where Oblivia Newton lives?" she asked.

Rick rejoined them at the patio table. "Hey, guys. There are two fishing boats coming into the harbor," he said. "We could ride our bikes down to the pier and pick up some fresh shrimp for dinner. Anybody up for that?"

Jason shook his head. His thoughts were elsewhere. "Rick, do you know where Oblivia lives?"

"Not a clue," Rick replied.

Jason leaned back in his chair, pushing a hand through his hair. "This is what I've got so far," he announced, and handed the paper to Rick.

1. *Get the map back from Oblivia.*

2. *Discover what's on that map — even before finding it!*

3. *Learn EVERYTHING there is to know about the Door to Time.*

4. *Search all of Argo Manor, from top to bottom.*

"Easier said than done," Rick said, handing the list back to Jason. Rick settled into a chair. "So what's the plan?"

"We have to do all this," Jason said, "in one day."

"What's the hurry?" Julia wondered.

"Mom and Dad are coming back tonight," Jason reminded the others. "Rick needs to get back home."

The boy from Kilmore Cove's face instantly darkened. He didn't want to return home. Not now. Not yet.

"We need to put something else on that list," Julia said. "We really don't know what happened to . . ." Julia limited herself to just pointing toward the cliffs, hoping that the boys would understand.

Rick nodded in silent agreement.

Jason added three words to the bottom of the page:

5. *Find Manfred's body.*

They heard a long, rattling series of coughs. Moments later, Nestor appeared from around the corner. He was pushing a wheelbarrow loaded with an assortment of gardening tools. He began the long, slow, tedious job of picking up the fallen debris from the white gravel.

"I didn't see anything down at the beach," he muttered aloud, as if answering an unspoken question. "No body, no Manfred. The fall must have carried him beyond the rocks and into the water. A very lucky man," Nestor said. "Like a cat with nine lives." He bent over and sneezed loudly.

Julia watched him with concern. He was, after all, just an old man. Last night had taken a lot out of him. "We need to get Nestor some medicine," she whispered to the boys.

"Today is Sunday," Rick reminded her. "Dr. Bowen's office is closed."

"I don't need medicine," Nestor grumbled. "It's just a simple cold, not the West Nile virus."

"It might be the flu," declared Julia. "Don't worry, it's our turn to take care of you."

Nestor waved the thought away. "I'm a tough old bird," he protested. "I won't be babied."

Jason suddenly turned to face Rick. "What did you say before?"

"I said that it's Sunday," Rick repeated. "The doctor's office . . ."

"Dr. Bowen," Jason repeated. "I've heard that name before. Or seen it somewhere . . ." He paused, wrinkling his forehead in concentration. "I've got it! It was on the back of the map! Bowen, Thomas Bowen!"

"What?" Rick said in surprise. "Really? But . . . how come you didn't mention it earlier?"

"There wasn't time — I barely had a chance to look at the map before Oblivia stole it from us." Jason's face darkened for a minute. "But it can't be a coincidence," he concluded. "We've got to check it out." Jason stood up, his body vibrating with energy. "Thomas Bowen could be the name of Dr. Bowen!"

Though Rick shared Jason's excitement, he was more realistic. "Or his great-great-grandfather," he said. "That looked like a very old map."

"Only one way to find out," Jason declared. "Let's go to his house right now!"

- Chapter 2 -
A PHONE CALL FROM LONDON

The ringing of the phone interrupted their plans. Mrs. Covenant was on the line. Jason was the first to speak with her.

"Yeah, Mom. No, Mom. Of course, Mom. No, we didn't stray far from the house. . . ."

He looked pleadingly at his sister, gesturing for her to take the phone. Julia smiled and shook her head, enjoying Jason's discomfort.

Rick whispered to Julia, "Your mother will be suspicious if you don't tell her anything. But if you give her a long, detailed story, she won't even listen to you."

Jason continued with his dull drone: "Uh-huh, yep, right, absolutely. What? No, nothing's going on. Nothing at all." Jason looked at Julia beseechingly. He held the phone at arm's length from his ear. His mother's voice, tinny and muffled, could still be heard.

"Okay, you want to know the truth?" Jason finally said, losing all patience. "Rick and I went to Egypt while Julia stayed home. We got lost in a labyrinth. Rick was almost eaten by a crocodile. Or an alligator. It's so hard to tell which is which. Anyway, you should have seen Rick's face when we entered that room filled with snakes!"

Jason stopped talking long enough to listen to his

mother. "I love you, too," he said. Then he handed the phone to Julia. "Your turn."

"Hi, Mom!" Julia exclaimed happily. "Oh yeah, we're absolutely fine. A little rain? Are you kidding? Buckets! We had a huge storm! Oh sure, we stayed indoors and played board games. I crushed the boys at Monopoly," she said, winking mischievously at Rick.

Jason and Rick drifted into the other room, as if bewitched by the Door to Time. The door was there, of course, tempting the boys to test themselves against its magic.

"When are we going back?" asked Rick in a hushed voice.

He didn't ask if, *he asked* when, Jason noted. "Soon," he replied. "But first, we need some answers."

Jason suddenly raised his hand, silencing his friend. He tilted his head, listening intently. "Did you hear that?"

Rick shook his head.

Jason rushed to the bottom of the stairs. He heard the sound of hurried footsteps coming from above.

"Now do you hear it?" he whispered to Rick.

Rick nodded emphatically. Yes, he heard it. Someone — or some*thing* — was upstairs.

Jason slowly climbed the stairs, trying to keep as quiet as possible. In the background, he could hear Julia happily prattling on into the phone: "We played chess, too. Naturally, I destroyed them. A total slaughter. Boys, you know. Nice enough to have around, but they aren't exactly the sharpest tools in the shed. . . ."

Jason was halfway up the stairs. *Ta-thump, ta-thump*. Ghost steps. Could it be . . . Ulysses Moore?

Keeping his back close to the wall, Jason brushed against the gold-framed portraits of the ancient owners that flanked the staircase. He continued up the stairs until he reached the blank spot where Ulysses Moore's portrait should have been.

Ta-thump, ta-thump. The sounds were coming from the bathroom, the first right at the top of the staircase, off the hallway that led to the bedrooms. Jason listened intently, trying to identify the exact source of the noise. On the left side of the staircase, a mirrored door led to the tower and the library.

Jason peered down through the rails of the banister and saw that Rick had remained immobile, staring worriedly at him. With a nod of his head, Jason reassured Rick that everything was all right. So far, so good. He could still hear Julia laughing on the phone.

Ta-thump, ta-thump. The intruder was behind the door. Jason took a deep breath and leaped toward the bathroom door. He threw it open, shouting, "Who are you?"

At first, the room appeared empty. Jason didn't notice anything unusual. Then he saw that the window was open. A few seconds later, a huge field rat made its way among the perfume bottles that Mrs. Covenant had placed on top of the sink. The rat, huge and disgusting, suddenly became aware of Jason's presence. It let out a horrible shriek, jumped to the tile floor, and scurried between Jason's feet.

Ta-thump, ta-thump.

Jason gave out an involuntary screech of surprise and jumped backward.

"Jason? What happened?!" yelled Rick, racing up the stairs.

On the way up Rick passed the rat, who was on its way down.

"Wha — ?"

"Did you see it?" Jason yelled from the top of the stairs.

"See it? How could I miss it?!" Rick answered. "That rat was the size of a house cat!"

Meanwhile, the terrified rodent was desperately trying to escape by sliding through the wrought-

iron spindles. Losing its grip, the feral creature fell to the floor with a dull thud, leaving it dazed.

The rat moved its head slightly, leaped up on all fours, and raced into the telephone room — where Julia sat unawares. "Aaaaack!" she shrieked, not so much out of fright, but out of shock.

Moments later, Jason was back on the phone, explaining the scene to his annoyed mother. "Yes, Mom. No, Mom. Of course I didn't do it on purpose. No, it wasn't a joke!" he protested. "It was a rat — a really big rat. You should have seen it, Mom. It was like the size of a pony! No, I have no idea what a rat was doing in the bathroom. I think it came in through the window."

While Jason worked to soothe his mother's concerns, Rick and Julia poked around the living room with two long brooms, searching for the revolting rodent. Each wore a unique expression: Rick, one of amusement; Julia, pure disgust.

"Oh hi, Dad. Yeah, we're fine — except for this gigantic rat," Jason told his father. "It's like the size of King Kong. I'm going to contact the people at the *Guinness Book of World Records* right after we get off the phone," he said, laughing. "What? Really? You can't make it back tonight? Yes!"

He pumped a fist in the air, then shot Rick and Julia the *v* sign for victory.

"I mean, um," he continued, "that's really too bad. We'll miss you. But, um, we're okay. Don't worry. Everything's cool."

Rick and Julia stopped their search. They were suddenly very interested in Jason's conversation.

"No problem!" Jason said, giving Julia a big thumbs-up. "We'll take care of it. Nestor? He's way on the other side of the garden. Try calling back at dinnertime," Jason suggested. "He'll be around for sure. Don't worry, we'll be fine. See you, Dad. Have a safe trip."

Click. Jason hung up the phone. "Yes!" he roared. "Awesome! They won't be back until tomorrow morning at the earliest!"

"That's so great!" Julia exclaimed.

"Now we'll have enough time to take care of things," Jason said.

Rick agreed. "First let me call my mom," he said. "As long as I check in with her, I'm sure I can stay with you guys all day."

After Rick called home, he and Jason quickly went over the last-minute details. They'd get the bikes, pack some lunches, then . . .

"There you are!" Julia screamed.

Wham, whack, blam!

The boys turned to look at Julia.

She had slammed the broom on the ground. "Boys,"

she said with a triumphant smirk, "that is one very big, and now very dead, rat."

Stepping out the front door, they found Nestor still busy with his chores, gathering the leaves and branches and throwing them in the wheelbarrow.

"Did you come out to help me clean up the yard?" Nestor asked, half-teasingly.

"Sorry, Nestor, but we have to go somewhere," Jason answered. "My parents called. The move is taking longer than they expected. They said they won't be back until tomorrow at the earliest."

Nestor gave no outward reaction, but Julia noticed that his eyes seemed to twinkle ever so slightly. "Yeah, it's a real bummer . . . NOT!" she said, grinning at him.

"Hold on," Nestor said. "Where do you think you're going?"

"We're going to find Dr. Bowen," Julia answered.

Nestor bent down stiffly, dragging his rake across the gravel. Rick and Jason raced to the garage to get the bikes.

Julia stepped closer to Nestor. She felt a new connection to him, a closeness brought on by the experience they had shared the night before. "Is your back okay?" she asked.

"My mood is in worse shape than my back," he replied. "I keep thinking about last night. If it had been just a few years ago, things would have gone very differently. Trust me."

That's when Julia understood. His pride was hurt. Nestor felt that he had failed to protect her from Manfred, and he was ashamed.

"You were great," Julia said reassuringly. She planted a swift, unexpected kiss on his cheek. "So brave and, um, brave!" she said.

Even Nestor had to laugh at that. He paused, leaning on his rake. "To grow old, Julia, it is a terrible thing. You lose your strength, your energy. You become tired, feeble. Yes, it's a terrible thing." He smiled at Julia. "I advise against it."

"Right," Julia answered with a nod. "But I guess it beats the alternative."

"Food for worms?" Nestor replied. "You can cremate me, dear Julia. I do not wish to ever be buried and become a smorgasbord for hundreds of worms!"

"Gosh, you really *are* in a bad mood today," Julia teased.

Nestor jerked his head in the direction of Rick and Jason, who were hustling over toward them. "Their mood is going to be even worse, I'm afraid."

Nestor was right. The boys looked miserable.

They were dragging the bicycles along and wearing unhappy expressions. "Who did this?" Rick asked. "It looks like somebody took a hammer to the bikes."

"They're ruined!" Jason said with fury in his voice. "How did this happen?"

Julia instantly guessed the answer. Manfred. Prowling around the house the night before, frustrated and angry, he delighted in causing damage.

"It was Manfred," she explained. "We couldn't do anything to stop him."

Nestor hung his head, deep in thought — or perhaps in shame.

"It's not your fault," Rick said.

"No," said Jason. "It was Oblivia Newton. She's the one behind all this. She's the one who keeps getting in our way."

His hands tightened into fists, then went white — bloodless — from squeezing so hard.

Rick laid the bikes on the gravel with the care of a surgeon examining a patient on the operating table. Tools were neatly lined on the ground, as if placed there by a competent nurse, awaiting surgery.

"Let's see," Rick murmured, examining the damaged bicycles from all angles. He frowned. "This is going to take some time."

Jason and Julia stood to the side, feeling useless. Jason was brilliant, in his own way, but he lacked practical skills. His head was usually in the clouds, and that's not where mechanical repairs are made. Julia, for her part, had never once given the slightest thought to the inner workings of a bicycle. She had no more interest in fixing a bike than she had in splitting the atom. When things broke, you bought a new one. No fuss, no muss. Easy.

"Is it really that bad?" she asked.

"Yeah," Rick answered with a tight smile. "It really, really is that bad. This will take at least an hour."

Jason nodded gloomily. He wanted to get started right now. "Can I help?" he asked.

Rick chuckled. "Do you know what a screwdriver looks like, Jason?"

"Well, yeah, of course." Jason scanned the tools, as if looking at them for the first time. "Um, it's that kind of pointy one, I think. . . ."

"Wow," Rick said with a smile. "Very impressive, Jason. But to be honest with you guys, it will be faster if I do this myself."

Jason was relieved. He turned and gazed at Argo Manor, that place of wonder and hidden secrets. He said to Rick, "While you, um, mess around with this stuff, Julia and I will explore more of the house."

"Great," said Rick. His concentration was already fixed on the task before him.

Julia seemed to hesitate for a moment, staying close to Rick. "Are you coming, Julia?" Jason asked.

For some reason, Julia was in no hurry to go back into the house. For the first time since she'd arrived at Kilmore Cove, the house frightened her. She didn't know why. But the feeling nagged at her, like a warning in her ear, whispering that the house was dangerous.

"It's not a game," she snapped at Jason.

"What?"

"This whole thing," she said. "It's serious. People could get hurt."

Jason looked at his sister and nodded. "I know, Julia. We'll be careful," he promised. "It's not a game."

"Good," Julia said, satisfied. Yet at the same time, she chided herself for letting the mysterious house

get ahold of her. She was getting sucked into its strange spell. *I'm an idiot*, Julia thought. Jason was the dreamer, the one who read foolish comic books and imagined ghosts and goblins. Not her! She was the sensible one, with both feet firmly planted on the ground.

There's no reason to be afraid, she told herself. And she repeated it silently, over and over, as she and her twin entered the house.

Nothing to be afraid of ... nothing to be afraid of ... nothing to be ...

Julia and Jason went through the kitchen and into the dining room. Jason pushed aside the heavy drapes to let in more light. He studied the paintings on the walls. There were four paintings from the eighteenth century depicting, he soon realized, different scenes from the Old Testament. He opened the cast-iron doors of an old wood-burning stove. It was empty. He pulled open a drawer of a massive cupboard, the only piece of furniture in the room. It contained nothing but tablecloths and napkins. Boring.

"Nothing here," Jason said, disappointed.

"What did you expect, Lord Voldemort?" Julia joked.

Jason moved on to investigate the adjacent rooms. He thrust his head into the fireplace, moved several bookshelves, and looked under statues. Disheartened, he had to admit that the room had no secrets to reveal.

"I don't get it," Julia said. "What are we supposed to be looking for, anyway?"

"I'm not sure," Jason said. "Something we missed yesterday. Something we overlooked. There's got to be some sort of proof, like, I don't know — some papers, a journal, something."

"So we're snooping for clues," Julia surmised.

"Right," Jason answered.

"Okay," Julia said. "I'll be Velma, you can be Scooby-Doo."

"Ruh-roh," Jason joked, imitating the cartoon canine.

They moved into another room, pulling open drawers, looking under furniture. At Jason's request, Julia repeated everything that Nestor had revealed to her about the exotic travels of Ulysses Moore.

"He said that Oblivia Newton was a mistake. A terrible mistake," Julia said. "But I don't think he knows anything more about it."

Jason raised his eyebrows and tilted his head, uncertain whether to agree or not. "I don't know," he said. "But if Nestor has any answers, he sure is tight-lipped about them."

They had entered the stone room. And there they stopped, without speaking, before the Door to Time.

"If you're looking for answers, you can find them behind that door," said Julia, shivering involuntarily.

Jason bent down and picked up a few grains of sand from the floor. "These prove we're not crazy," he whispered, showing them to Julia.

After a pause, he asked, "Do you have the keys?"

Julia patted her pocket and nodded.

"Give them to me."

Julia was reluctant. She said, "Nestor told me that the door will reopen only if whoever entered has returned."

"Well? We're back, aren't we?" Jason pointed out.

"I know, but what about Oblivia?"

"There's only one way to find out," Jason said. He put the first key into the top keyhole: Owl. Then he inserted the second and third keys: Porcupine and Elephant.

"O-P-E . . ." Julia whispered.

Jason inserted the fourth key into the bottom lock: Newt.

"Open," Julia said.

Jason turned the final key. *Click, clack, click, click.* And the door swung slowly open.

They stood motionless on the threshold. Beyond

lay a round room, its walls covered in coded writings, palindromes. Adjusting their eyes to the darkness, the twins discerned exits at the end of each of three passageways leading below. One passageway, they knew, led to the subterranean grotto where the *Metis* was docked.

"Manfred had a key like ours," Julia said. "Before he fell, he snatched it from the air. . . ."

"But it was just one key," Jason said hopefully. "Do you think he wanted to get inside Argo Manor to use the key?"

Julia shook her head uncertainly. "So much happened last night, Jason. I'm not sure what he wanted, exactly."

"What does Nestor think?" Jason asked.

"Nestor told me that it was a copy of Argo Manor's key," Julia said. "All I know for sure is that he was prepared to die to keep Manfred from getting that key."

Jason nodded his head solemnly.

"Do you believe the old man?" he asked his sister.

"Yes, Jason. I do."

Jason made a face. "Yesterday, you didn't trust him at all!"

"Jason, you weren't here! You don't know what happened. Nestor risked his life to save the house,"

Julia said, becoming agitated. "Manfred was crazed, dangerous. And at that time, I felt absolutely sure that Nestor was on our side."

"I guess," Jason said. "But he's so secretive. He only gives us little bits and pieces."

"Everything he's told us has been true," Julia countered.

"Look, Julia," Jason said. "You're right. I wasn't here last night. If I was, maybe I'd feel differently. But right now, I still don't fully trust him. Not one hundred percent."

"You still don't think Ulysses Moore is dead, do you?" Julia asked.

"I don't know what to believe, Julia. That's why I want proof — one way or the other," Jason confided. "I'm so angry that Oblivia stole that map from us. I'm sure it held important clues." Jason held his hand before his face. "We had it, but it slipped through our fingers. And now I don't know where to turn."

Jason peered into the darkness of the round room.

He said, "I wonder if the ship came back to the dock. I wonder if the fireflies are circling the grotto."

He took a step forward.

Julia reached out to stop him. "Jason," she warned. "If we go beyond the threshold, we may be forced to board the *Metis* again."

"How can you know that?" he asked.

"We don't know how it works," Julia said. "That's all I'm saying. Are you ready to take that risk?"

Jason lowered his head, using his foot to draw an imaginary line on the floor. "So, this is the farthest we can go before passing into a different world, another time. If we take one more step, we . . ."

Julia pulled Jason back into the stone room. She closed the door gently but firmly.

"Not now," she said. "Not yet. First, there's your list. And Rick. Plus we still have business in Kilmore Cove at Dr. Bowen's."

Jason cheered up at the thought. "Yes," he agreed. "Maybe we'll find answers there."

With Rick still busy repairing the bicycles, Jason and Julia climbed the stairs to the second floor. They went directly to the library.

To Julia, though the library was magnificent, it had an ominous feeling, as if she were walking into a burial vault, a sacred place for old relics. Maybe it was the dark, heavy bookcases. The crowded furniture. Or the painted ceiling, like something you'd find in a great Italian chapel. For whatever reason, the room spooked her. She took solace in the view from the windows. The trees in the garden swaying

in the constant sea breeze; the gravel courtyard; the entrance gate. Outside the window, she saw light and life. Inside the library . . . it was a tomb, a resting place for the past.

In the center of the room, there was a bronze chandelier in the shape of a heron suspended from the ceiling. Beneath it were a crystal table, a buffalo skin sofa, and a pair of stuffed chairs.

Jason looked in awe at the ancient gold-leaf books. They immediately seemed precious, valuable, rare. One entire bookcase was marked PALEOGRAPHY. That's where the kids had found and removed the *Dictionary of Forgotten Languages.* It had served them well. Maybe they could find something useful this time around, too.

"To understand this place," Jason said, "we first need to learn about its history."

"Nestor said this room has the genealogical tree of the Moore family," Julia told Jason. She looked around, blowing a few strands of hair out of her face. "Thing is, he didn't say where, exactly."

After a short search, Jason opened a glass case. He found a series of small books tied together with a black ribbon. A number was printed in golden letters on the spine of each volume.

He untied the ribbon and examined one of the

books. It didn't appear to have a title. After turning a few blank pages, Jason found a drawing of a heavily stylized family tree. He turned the page and saw an old photo of a stern-looking man wearing a British army uniform. He had an enormous white mustache that immediately reminded Julia of a walrus. In the background of the photo, there was an elephant tusk. A caption identified the man as Mercury Malcolm Moore and included the dates of his birth and death. He had died nearly a hundred years ago.

Stuffed inside the book was a packet of old papers. To keep them from getting damaged, the documents were separated by onionskin paper. There were also old postmarked letters, exotic writings, and canceled stamps. Jason was transported. These old documents, photos, and letters appealed to his imagination. It was as if he were holding a treasure.

Julia looked over his shoulder and frowned. "Just a bunch of old junk," she concluded. Then she added, "It looks like he lived in India or somewhere like that."

In the next section, they found photos of Thomas and Annabelle Moore, who wore old-fashioned hunting gear. Accompanying these photos was a batch of letters and official documents — birth certificates and such.

Jason grabbed another slender black book from the case and began skimming through it. He found other names and documents, all meticulously classified and carefully — no, *lovingly* — tied together.

The twins settled onto the sofa to read, becoming absorbed in the stories of these strangers. "It must have taken forever to organize all this stuff," Jason noted. "Just an amazing effort, keeping all this history alive and in one place."

"Yeah, it's cool," Julia said.

"But it's not a true genealogical tree," Jason said. "I want to see it all in one place. This is more like a giant, sprawling scrapbook than a true family tree."

Jason felt a tap on his shoulder. Then harder, more insistent. "What, Julia?" he snapped, not looking up.

Julia kept tapping.

Irritated, Jason turned to see what her problem was. His sister's eyes were glued to the ceiling. "Look, Jason."

Jason lifted his eyes to examine the painted ceiling. And there it was — somehow they hadn't noticed it until that moment. On the ceiling there was a vast painting. Five large medallions were strung together through the branches of a great tree. There were drawings of animals and strange fruit on every branch, all identified by name.

"This is it!" Jason exclaimed. He excitedly read some of the names: "Cantarellus Moore, Tiberius Moore, Adriana Moore, Xavier Moore . . ."

At the top of the tree, there were two branches, only two names. On each branch sat a white seagull. The names were, of course, Ulysses and Penelope. The last of the long line of Moores. The end of the tree.

"Stunning," Julia murmured.

Using the great painting as a reference point, Julia and Jason quickly found the names of the people in the small, black, leather-bound books. "It's like an index, a reference tool," Julia said in awe.

"Look," Jason exclaimed. He pointed to the roots that dug into one of the five medallions. "The Moore family tree grows from out of the turtle's back. Again with that symbol!"

"What do you mean, *again*?" Julia inquired.

"Don't you remember? It's the symbol on the grotto's entrance. It was also in the Land of Punt, in the Room That Isn't There. It was at the feet of the Founders' statues."

Julia blinked and tapped the side of her head. "Sorry, Jason, but you just lost me. The Founders?"

"Look at the medallions, Julia," Jason said, pointing. "Inside each medallion is a picture of an animal. Do they look familiar to you?"

"Owl . . . porcupine . . . elephant . . . newt," Julia said in a shivery whisper. "The same as on the keys to the door."

Elsewhere on the ceiling, Jason discovered a rendering of the *Metis*, sailing alongside another vessel. "I've seen that one before," he told Julia. "In the tower. Come with me."

Jason quickly left the room, heading directly to the tower. He did not bother to check to see if Julia was following. Jason pushed open the tower room's mirrored door and entered.

The tower was exactly the same as Nestor had left it the previous night. The old caretaker had made sure that the broken window was fixed, although a draft still leaked through the cracks. The manuscripts and journals were stacked on the floor, and the model ships were on the box seat by a window. Jason picked up the model of *Nefertiti's Eye*, thinking of the Great Master Scribe who had built it, Maruk's father. He reviewed the others: a piragua, a gondola, a galleon. Why were some of these vessels painted on the family tree? Jason racked his brain, searching for an answer. What was the logic behind it? There must be a reason for everything.

Julia caught up with her brother. She stood by the window, watching him with a mixture of admiration and amusement. She knew that at times like these, her brother was virtually possessed. The best thing for her to do would be to step back and let him go. He would come back to earth eventually.

Julia could see Rick in the courtyard below. She got his attention by banging on the glass. Rick waved and called, "I'm almost finished! Come on down!"

She tugged on Jason's sleeve, jarring him from his reverie. "Time to go, Jason."

"Huh? What?"

"You're so weird sometimes. . . ." Julia commented, rolling her eyes. "Let's hit the road."

- Chapter 4 -
NO BRAKES

The sun was already high in the sky. The day was slipping away. Rick had one of the bicycles upside down. He was testing the gears and brakes, and he didn't seem pleased. Nestor continued working, but periodically cast a furtive eye toward the kids.

"We ready to roll?" Jason asked Rick.

Rick shrugged. "I don't totally trust the brakes on this one," he said, gesturing toward the old bicycle that used to be Mrs. Moore's. "It doesn't seem safe."

"I'll ride it," Jason offered.

"No, that's okay," Julia said. "I'm a good rider. I should be the one."

"Don't argue, Julia," Jason countered. "I said I'll ride the bike. It's settled."

Julia just shook her head, surprised by Jason's forcefulness. Boys could be so old-fashioned. Jason still wanted to be her protector, her "big" brother, even though she was every inch as tough and capable as he was. But she had to admit, it was sort of sweet. And, well, that old bike did look like a hunk of junk.

Nestor hobbled up to the kids. He gruffly asked, "Where are you going?"

Julia eyed the old man. He looked weary, exhausted, sick. His eyes were glassy, and his cough was thick and rumbling. "You should take it easy today," Julia said.

Nestor waved the thought away. "Work is good," he said. "I'm fine. It's just a little cold."

"Um, Nestor?" Jason said. "Do you know where Dr. Bowen lives?"

"No."

"What about Oblivia Newton?"

Nestor wiped sweat from his forehead. "Do I look like a tour guide to you? I'm just the caretaker here."

"I thought you knew everyone in Kilmore Cove," Jason protested.

"You thought wrong," Nestor shot back. Then he turned back to his work.

Rick sighed heavily. Nothing was ever easy. So he put down his bicycle and went inside Argo Manor. He returned two minutes later, a look of satisfaction on his face. "Dr. Bowen lives in a cottage on Hummingbird Alley. It's toward the very end of Salton Cliff, on the right," he announced.

"How did you find that out?" Nestor asked.

"I called my mom," Rick answered. "Very handy to have around."

Nestor rubbed his chin. "Yes, perhaps a phone can be useful from time to time — but I'll never like them."

Rick laughed. "I was talking about my mother, not the telephone; *she* can be useful from time to time!"

Julia looked crossly at Nestor. "You knew where he lives," she contended. "Why wouldn't you tell us?"

Nestor opened his mouth, hesitated, then shut it, as if changing his mind. "I don't believe in taking medicine for every little sniffle," he grumbled. "There's no need for you kids to ride all that way."

"Oh sure!" said Jason. "Now I get it. You're afraid of doctors!"

Jason hopped on Mrs. Moore's bicycle and pedaled toward the wrought-iron gate. Julia and Rick followed.

"Be careful," Nestor called to them. He coughed heavily, bracing himself against his rake. When he looked up, the bicycles were already out of sight. "Just be careful," he repeated softly.

"WAH-HOOOO!" Jason screamed, whizzing ahead of the others along the Salton Cliff road. "THIS BIKE IS SO WOBBLY!" he yelled.

Julia laughed happily. It felt good to be moving her muscles, biking in the fresh air. But Rick was worried that Jason was too reckless. He called after him to slow down.

"I CAN'T," Jason called back. "THE BRAKES DON'T WORK SO GOOD."

Julia shot Rick a concerned look. "I thought you fixed it," she said.

"I warned him," Rick answered, pedaling faster now. "He wouldn't listen."

That right there, Julia mused, was their relationship in a nutshell. Rick, the practical one, the voice of reason. Jason was more . . . spiritual. Whimsical, reckless; he trusted his feelings more than he trusted his brain. It was, she reflected, a good way to get yourself killed.

They came upon a series of three hairpin turns. Rick watched Jason up ahead. He seemed under control — as long as the bike stayed in one piece.

"Stay back," Rick advised Julia. "Keep your speed down and be careful on these curves. I'll try to catch up with Jason." He rose on his pedals, pushing harder, picking up speed, trying to close the distance between him and Jason. Then Rick crouched low over the handlebars, gliding as he gained momentum. He was perfectly in sync with his bicycle. The cliffs disappeared behind him, white and silent, while the houses of Kilmore Cove loomed closer at each bend.

Rick saw Jason approaching the third and final hairpin turn. He was going too fast, yet he still

howled out loud with a mixture of panic and exhilaration. But Rick had to concentrate on the road. He couldn't help Jason. Rick reluctantly squeezed the brakes, gently applying more pressure as his bike slowed down. He couldn't catch Jason; it was too dangerous, and it wouldn't do any good even if he could. Rick looked back over his shoulder. Julia was getting closer. He signaled for her to slow down. "I think Bowen's house is just behind that turn, immediately on your right!" he called. "Hummingbird Alley."

Julia nodded. "Let's hope Jason sees it."

As Rick and Julia made it around the bend, they saw Jason's bicycle in a ditch, its wheels spinning wildly in the air.

Rick pulled to a stop and leaped off his bike. Jason lay on the grass a short distance away.

Julia's heart was in her throat. She cried, "JASON! ARE YOU ALL RIGHT?!"

Jason turned to look at them. He was smiling like a lunatic. "I pulled a Fred Flintstone!" he exclaimed. His pants and polo shirt were covered with grass and dirt stains. He appeared to have scratches on his arms and face. But mostly, he looked . . . happy. No broken bones.

"The brakes weren't working, so I tried to slow down by using my feet," Jason explained, dusting himself off.

"Like Fred Flintstone?" Julia said.

"Right," Jason answered brightly.

"Great," said Julia. "You're taking cycling lessons . . . from a cartoon about a prehistoric caveman! That's brilliant, Jason."

Jason smiled goofily. "Hey, it worked." He noticed the damaged bicycle. "Sort of."

Rick was relieved. The gate was made of wood, painted blue, and designed with a floral arrangement in the shape of a large letter *b*. A nearby street sign read: HUMMINGBIRD ALLEY.

"We're here," Rick said. "This must be Dr. Bowen's house."

- Chapter 5 -
NESTOR MAKES A CALL

After the kids were gone, Nestor entered his private cottage. Once inside, he locked the door, closed the curtains, and walked toward his old-fashioned black telephone. He disliked using it. Hated it, in fact. And yet, the time had come to make the call. Things were escalating quickly, and getting nasty.

After he heard how Oblivia had stolen the map, Nestor could not get the thought out of his head that he had made a terrible mistake — a mistake that could not be fixed.

Based on what the kids had told him, there were still many things that didn't make sense. For instance, why was the map not where it was supposed to have been? Who moved it to the Room That Isn't There? Why was the passage to the Door to Time sealed by an outside wall?

No one had said anything to him.

There was one possible answer: Oblivia. Perhaps she had a hand in it. But again, that didn't seem quite right. According to Jason and Rick, Oblivia was angry when she discovered that the niche of the four wands was empty.

What now? he wondered. Things were not going the way he expected. Something was fundamentally different. The rules of the game had changed.

Nestor picked up the telephone. His fingers were numb, as often happened when he was worried. Finally, he dialed.

"Homer and Homer Movers," answered the secretary.

"I wish to speak with the proprietor, please," Nestor said.

"The owner is unavailable at the moment," the secretary droned. "May I take a message?"

"It is a matter of great importance," Nestor replied.

"I'm sorry," the nasal voice answered. "But . . ."

"Please," Nestor pleaded. "Tell him that it . . . regards the property of Mr. Moore."

The secretary seemed to hesitate, responding to something in Nestor's voice. "I'll see what I can do," she relented.

After a few minutes, Homer answered the phone. He spoke quickly, as if he had something else to do. "I was wondering when you'd call," Homer said. "Things on my end are getting complicated. I can't hold the Covenants off much longer. They are getting frustrated, to say the least."

"Do whatever you must," Nestor stated flatly. "Just delay them for as long as possible."

"No can do," Homer replied. "If we continue to

go on like this, they'll call another firm to handle the move."

"I'll double your fee," Nestor said.

"Hmmm," Homer said, pausing a beat. "It's a deal."

"One last thing," Nestor said. "If you see the Covenants are intent on returning sooner, you must call me. Do you understand?"

"Yes, of course I understand. You're the boss," Homer said snarkily.

"Don't call me that," Nestor snapped irritably.

"Sure . . . boss," Homer replied.

Nestor slammed the phone onto the receiver. That man was irritating, but sufficiently motivated by money not to ask too many questions. On the other hand, who would pay a moving company double their fee to make the move as slow as possible?

Nestor paced around the room pensively. Again, he picked up the telephone. He knew the number by heart, even after all these years.

A man's voice, low and deep, answered.

"What is it?"

"Hello, Leonard," Nestor said. His tone was much more friendly than it had been with Homer.

On the other end of the phone, there was a long moment of silence.

"It has been a long time since I last spoke with you," Nestor continued.

"Yes, a long time," answered Leonard Minaxo, Kilmore Cove's lighthouse keeper. "To be honest with you, I preferred it that way."

"The keys are back," Nestor said. His tone was neutral, without threat or emotion. As if he were talking about any ordinary thing. The sky is blue. The leaves are falling. The keys are back.

Leonard Minaxo caught his breath. "How many?"

"I'm positive four are in our possession. One is currently missing. And another has likely fallen into the wrong hands."

"Who put them in the game again?" the light-house keeper demanded.

"I don't know," Nestor said. "Who, why, what, when. All I know is that the keys have returned to Kilmore Cove."

"Who has the keys?" Leonard asked.

"Three children," Nestor answered, "and the thief."

"Are the children making progress?" Leonard asked.

"Yes," Nestor answered. "They are smart, resourceful. There may be hope."

- Chapter 6 -
ON THE TRAIL OF THE MAP

An old woman's brittle voice answered the intercom. When the three children asked to see Dr. Bowen, a buzzer opened the gate leading them onto an impeccably kept white gravel path.

"It's the seven dwarfs," whispered Julia, noting the ceramic statues in the doctor's immaculate garden. There was a swing with pink bows tied on the rope, a well with a tiny pail attached to a chain, and a decorative wheelbarrow brimming with purple periwinkles.

The woman greeted them at the door. She opened the door wide, to the delicate sound of chimes, and gestured for the kids to step inside. Julia, always observant, saw that the woman was unusually pale, almost colorless. As if to counter the drabness of her appearance, her hair was extravagantly coiffed. She held in her hands two pairs of disposable light blue slippers, but as soon as she saw the three kids, she exclaimed, "Oh mercy!" She made an abrupt, panicked turn, and hustled inside to fetch a third pair of slippers.

Jason and Rick took a small step back, leaving Julia the honor of introducing them.

"Good morning, Mrs. Bowen," Julia said kindly. "We're so awfully sorry to disturb you. Is your husband at home?"

"No bother, my dearies," the woman answered

warmly. "As a doctor's wife, I've grown used to comings and goings at all hours of the day." She handed them the slippers, nodding conspiratorially. "Would you mind terribly putting on these slippers before entering? Germs, you know."

Her guests did not mind, and gladly put on the slippers.

Mrs. Bowen examined each one in turn. "What happened to you, dearie?" she asked Jason, looking anxiously at his cuts and bruises.

Jason was glad to have an audience, and thoroughly enjoyed retelling every detail of his triumphant tumble.

Mrs. Bowen shook her head and clucked, "Good heavens! Please wait one moment!" She went deeper into the house.

"That hairdo makes her look like a mushroom," Jason murmured. Julia gave him a sharp elbow in rebuke, but couldn't help agreeing silently. Mrs. Bowen did look a lot like a mushroom, now that Jason mentioned it.

Mrs. Bowen reappeared with a white disposable paper robe. She offered it to Jason. "Please put this on," she said. And again added in a hushed whisper, "Germs — can't have them running roughshod all over the house."

Jason took the robe with the tips of his fingers, as

if he were a doctor preparing for surgery. He followed the others inside the Bowens' cottage, mumbling sarcastically to himself, "I didn't hurt myself when I fell, really — but thanks for asking."

The inside of the house was so clean and polished that the kids almost needed sunglasses to shield their eyes from the blinding glare. The furniture was scarce and oddly mismatched. The bright tabletops were made of glass and aluminum, cold and futuristic. Instead of Argo Manor's antique lamps, dark crystal, and brass chandeliers, this house had small iridescent lights poking out of the ceilings like dozens of little aliens tunneling into the house.

Dr. Bowen — a kind-looking middle-aged man — sat in the living room, reading.

"Good morning," he greeted the children in a friendly voice. "What brings you to my home on a Sunday morning?"

Mrs. Bowen, her hands fluttering like two small sparrows, informed her husband what had happened before the kids could get a word in edgewise. After finishing her account of their adventure, she looked at them expectantly, as if waiting for their approval for getting all the essential details correct.

"Is the bicycle broken?" asked the doctor, a twinkle in his eyes.

"To put it lightly," Rick replied. "Destroyed is more like it."

"A shame," the doctor noted.

"Yes, but I didn't get hurt!" Jason proudly reminded everyone. "And I did stop at the right place."

"Oh yes, the best place for a smashup — right outside a doctor's door!" said Dr. Bowen with an easy laugh. "Edna?" he said, turning to his wife. "Don't we still have our daughter's bike in the garage?"

"Certainly," Mrs. Bowen answered. "I stored it safely to keep it in good condition."

Dr. Bowen smiled to himself, gently amused. "Our daughter, you see," he explained to his guests, "is forty-one years old and lives in London. I hardly expect that she'll get much use of it anymore." The doctor looked intently at his wife. "I'm sure we could lend it to the boy."

"Well," the old woman said, clearly agitated. Her fluttery hands went to her hair, smoothed her dress, danced in the air. "I suppose . . . of course, there's no reason . . ."

"Good," the doctor said with a forced smile. "Why don't you get it for our guests. I'll entertain them while you are gone."

Mrs. Bowen opened her mouth to argue, but her husband had turned his attention to Jason. His mind

was made up, and the matter was closed. Mrs. Bowen made an indignant pirouette and marched out of the room.

Dr. Bowen waited until he heard the outside door open and close. He eyed the children suspiciously. "So what brings you to my humble home this fine morning?"

"It's Nestor, the caretaker at Argo Manor," Julia explained. "He's not feeling well. He, um, coughs like crazy, sneezes up a storm, and his eyes are all watery," she explained.

Jason and Rick nodded in agreement.

"It would probably be best if you could take a look at him," Jason suggested.

Dr. Bowen let out a booming laugh.

"A look! At Nestor? Ah, ha-ha! Name me one doctor that's been able to do that! I don't think I've sold even one aspirin to anyone who ever lived in Argo Manor," the doctor said. "In fact, wait, hold on a minute," he corrected himself. "That's not so. There was a time when the caretaker did buy sunscreen lotion. He claimed it was for Mrs. Moore."

Again, he laughed heartily, as if he'd just said something funny.

"I remember because he bought the strongest sunscreen on the market," the doctor said. "Mrs. Moore must have had very sensitive skin to get a sunburn in cloudy Kilmore Cove!"

"I guess so," Jason answered tensely.

"Another time," the doctor added, warming to his subject, "Nestor came to me for an anti-viper serum. That's right! Where on earth would they find a poisonous snake in Kilmore Cove? What goes on up at that house, I wonder?" the doctor said, eyes gleaming. He clapped his hands together. "So, as I said, it will be very difficult for me to offer Nestor my services, since he will only refuse them. Don't you agree? Now, how's his disposition?"

"His . . . disposition?" Julia echoed doubtfully.

Dr. Bowen laughed. "I mean, is he still a grouchy old fellow? Or has he gotten even worse?"

"He's actually pretty nice," Julia said, defending Nestor. "You just have to get to know him."

"That Nestor is from the old school," continued Dr. Bowen, not unkindly. "There are still many like him — some of these old folks living around here. He trusts neither doctors nor medicine. I suspect it stems from his leg, which was never repaired correctly. You've seen the limp, of course? Well, that's what we call one of life's bad breaks. The bones were not set correctly and, thus, never healed properly."

"You think he's angry about that?" Rick asked.

The doctor shrugged. "Who knows? Even with a bad leg, nothing seems to slow him down. He'll work all day, every day, on that house."

"It sounds like you know him pretty well," Julia observed.

The good doctor shifted in his seat. "Nestor would bicycle into town to run his errands," he said. "We spoke then and, yes, I suppose we became friends of a sort over the years. I never once went there to see him."

"You never went up to Argo Manor?" Jason asked, surprised.

"Oh, I went up there," Dr. Bowen replied, "but I was never invited inside. Very private, very particular, the Moores. Edna and I used to hike these hills, and sometimes we'd stop at Argo Manor's gate, chat with Nestor about this and that and the other thing. He gave us gardening advice, mostly. Occasionally, we'd glimpse the Moores from a distance, whenever they were down on their private beach."

"What kind of people were they?" Rick asked, eager to hear more.

"They kept to themselves," Dr. Bowen replied. "Not friendly, but not unfriendly, either. To be honest, it was as if they didn't live in Kilmore Cove. They were just private folks, I think, who wanted to be left alone."

While Dr. Bowen was talking about the Moores, Jason looked around the room. He tried to find anything that would link this mild doctor, sunk deep into the overstuffed sofa, to the map he had recovered in the Land of Punt. But no matter how hard he looked, Jason only saw crocheted doilies and other trinkets on the walls and shelves.

He finally spoke up. "There's another reason why we came to see you," he confessed.

The doctor smiled politely, waiting.

"Does the name Thomas Bowen mean anything to you?"

"Thomas Bowen?" the doctor repeated. He leaned his head back, closed his eyes briefly, and thought. "Yes, I have an ancestor with that name."

Jason glanced at Rick and Julia, trying to conceal his excitement from the doctor.

"He was an odd sort of a character," Dr. Bowen recalled. "A cartographer, if I remember correctly."

"A mapmaker," Rick said in a hushed voice.

"That's him!" Jason blurted out, no longer able to contain himself.

Dr. Bowen looked at him, flabbergasted. "You know of Thomas Bowen? Well, you might be interested to learn this was once his house."

"Incredible!" Rick cried out.

"Did you . . . somehow save some of his works . . . maybe some maps?" Jason asked hopefully.

"No, no, of course not," the doctor answered without hesitation. "You've already met my wife, Edna. She has her phobias, I must admit. Edna would not cotton to living in a home cluttered with dusty relics. Germs and clutter, those are Edna's mortal enemies. So we threw everything away."

Jason slumped into a chair. He stammered, "B-b-but you can't throw away the past like that. . . ."

"Listen," Dr. Bowen said. "The original house was built during Napoleon Bonaparte's era. Napoleon — imagine that! When Edna and I moved here, we demolished the original house — it was just a shack, really — and we built this little villa with all the modern conveniences. That is, almost all, seeing that Kilmore Cove still isn't wired for cable, and no one can make the satellite TV work here on the coast."

Jason's paper robe crackled beneath his weight. "Are you absolutely sure that there's nothing left that belonged to Thomas Bowen?"

Dr. Bowen made a tossing gesture with his hands, "Out it went!" he claimed. "Everything *and* the kitchen sink, I might add!" He chuckled at his own joke.

"This is awful. Now I'm the one who is starting

to feel sick," Jason said to Julia. "I feel like I could throw up."

"Nice," Julia deadpanned. "Mrs. Bowen would just love that."

"What's the matter with him?" Dr. Bowen asked Julia.

"It's complicated," Julia answered, not sure how much she could reveal. "It's just that, well, we were hoping that we could get some information about a map that was drawn by your ancestor."

"It was a map of Kilmore Cove," Rick added.

"Oh, you must be talking about the one that hung in the kitchen!" announced the doctor, rising to his feet.

Jason eyes bugged out. "In the kitchen?!"

The doctor led them into the kitchen, a room so clean and sanitized that it could have been featured in *Better Homes and Gardens* magazine. The only item that looked out of place was a gold-framed watercolor of Kilmore Cove's bay that hung above the breakfast nook.

"It was right there," the doctor explained, "in the same spot as that painting. I remember that map well. It must have been drawn from the highest cliff, because you could see the entire coastline as well as the old houses of Kilmore Cove."

"That was it!" Jason thought with a shiver of regret. "What happened to it?"

The doctor scratched his head, a vacant expression on his face.

"Please try to remember," Jason urged. "It could be an important clue."

At that moment, Edna Bowen entered the kitchen. "The bicycle is ready," she said. Edna went to the sink and vigorously soaped her hands, scrubbing them furiously with a wire brush.

Weird, thought Julia.

"Edna, you arrived just in time," the doctor said to his wife. "Do you remember what happened to the map that hung in the kitchen?"

"That old thing? I most certainly do!" she retorted. "We gave it to the lighthouse keeper years ago. Or rather, to Penelope Moore!"

"Ah yes!" the doctor said, snapping his fingers. "You're right. That story about the shark bite! How could I have forgotten?"

The kids listened in anticipation.

Dr. Bowen smiled at his eager audience, enjoying their suspense. "Do you, by any chance, know the lighthouse keeper?" asked the good doctor.

"They don't," Rick answered. "Julia and Jason are new to Kilmore Cove. But I do. It's Mr. Minaxo."

Edna suddenly looked at the twins with new-found interest. "That's why I didn't recognize you," she said. "You're the twins from London!"

Julia smiled and made an exaggerated bow. "At your service," she replied.

"Roger, did you hear that?" Edna said to her husband. "These are the children of the family that bought Argo Manor. Gwendaline told me about them just yesterday when she did my hair."

Dr. Bowen chuckled, eyes twinkling. "Ah, Gwendaline. She's better than the newspaper when it comes to all the comings and goings about town," he noted. Then he congratulated Julia and Jason on their new house and welcomed them to Kilmore Cove.

"What about the lighthouse keeper?" Rick prodded, eager to return to the story.

Edna fastidiously dried her hands. "He came here with a horrible wound," she recalled, glancing at her husband. "He claimed that a shark bit him."

"In the eye," the doctor said, "and across the face. Very nasty business, indeed."

"It was on a Sunday, like this one," Edna recalled. "Of course, it was an emergency."

"Mrs. Moore brought him here," the doctor recalled. "Most unusual, I dare say. They arrived here on a sidecar from the cliffs below. She told me . . .

hmmm, what *did* she tell me? Ah yes! She told me that they had found him on the beach. It was a very delicate business, since he had gone into shock. I managed to stitch his cheek the best I could, though I'm just a country doctor, not a plastic surgeon. Leonard Minaxo is in good health today — although he lost the sight in one eye and, regrettably, boasts a remarkable scar across his face."

Dr. Bowen ran a finger from the inside corner of his eye, down his cheek, curving around to somewhere below his ear. "Not very pretty, I'm afraid," the doctor said.

Julia gulped. "Cool story, but what does it have to do with the map?" she asked.

"I'm getting to that," the doctor said patiently. "The following week the Moores returned here in their sidecar. A very rare visit, indeed. Ulysses stayed outside, solitary and aloof, all wrapped up in a white scarf. You could hardly see his face. He wore an old motorcycle helmet that looked like it had been retrieved from World War II. Mrs. Moore came in and brought me that painting you see on the wall. She said it was a gift of thanks."

Edna looked at it unhappily. "We couldn't turn it down. But really, it's not our style," she confessed. "But Mrs. Moore painted it herself. We could hardly say no."

Julia stepped closer to take a better look at the painting.

"So she painted this. . . ." Julia murmured, making an imaginary brushstroke in the air.

"Oh yes," Edna said. "She had talent, I must admit, even if I don't particularly care for the fine arts."

The doctor looked at the painting with a touch of melancholy. "Penelope was a lovely woman." He lowered his head. "So tragic that she is . . . gone."

"And the map?" Rick asked.

"The map, of course!" Dr. Bowen said. "We gave the map to Penelope in exchange for the painting!"

Edna nodded with satisfaction. "Clever, no? That way I was able to get rid of it!"

The kids looked at one another, trying to understand.

"Mind you, it was not a frivolous gift. Mrs. Moore had seen it in the kitchen while my husband was working on poor Mr. Minaxo. She was very keen on it. Oh, Mrs. Moore asked a thousand questions about that map. Any fool could see that she was very interested in it. So when she came to give us the painting, well, it was only fitting for us to offer her the map that she so admired."

"A fair exchange," the doctor pronounced. "Something from her family in exchange for something from our family."

Jason shook his head. He didn't understand what link there could possibly be between that map, Penelope Moore, and Oblivia Newton. With each new fact they learned, ten new questions arose.

"Why is everybody so interested in an old map of Kilmore Cove?" he murmured. "What is so special about it?"

"A very good question," the doctor replied. "Because you are not the only ones who have visited us here, asking about that map."

"What?" Jason said.

"The wealthy woman," the doctor answered. "Ms. Newton, I believe."

"She was here!" Jason exclaimed.

"Is she a friend?" Edna asked, surprised. "What a small world."

Rick smiled tightly, speaking up before the others. "Yes," he said. "A very small world. When was she here?"

"A month ago, more or less," Edna replied. "Ms. Newton said she had an interest in antiquities. She's in real estate, you know. Would have paid a pretty penny for it, too. If we had known it was so important, we would have never let it go."

"Ms. Newton said it was priceless," the doctor recalled. "One of a kind, she said. Isn't that right, Edna?"

The doctor's wife nodded in agreement.

"Do you happen to know where Ms. Newton lives?" Rick asked.

Edna shook her head. "Oh no. We don't travel in her circle," she said. "But I'd venture to guess that you can ask Gwendaline, in town. She knows Ms. Newton very well. Cuts her hair, of course. If anyone knows, it's Gwendaline."

"Well, she must live in Kilmore Cove," Jason concluded. "If she gets her hair done in town."

"I guess so," the doctor said. "Of course, how do we know if we, in fact, live in Kilmore Cove? Have you ever seen a sign that says KILMORE COVE?"

Rick looked puzzled. "Well, um, now that you mention it . . ."

"Of course you haven't," the doctor interrupted. "There is no sign. Where does Kilmore Cove begin? And where does it end? No one really knows!"

Edna reached out to touch Julia's arm. She patted her own hair and confided, girl to girl, that Julia really ought to give Gwendaline a try. "She'd do wonders for your hair," Edna said, frowning at Julia's scalp. "It's called the High Society Hair Salon — and she's open on Sundays."

At this, Edna looked down at the glistening floor, smiled at her reflection there, and patted her hair approvingly. "She really does a marvelous job."

Julia wasn't really listening. She was too intent upon the painting. It was good, she decided. But mostly, she tried to imagine the person who painted it, the artist behind the picture. What was she like? What did she feel? What did she fear? The picture itself was lovely, but not particularly unusual. It showed the bay of Kilmore Cove. A deep, vibrant sea. High-flying seagulls, like little commas, and the outline of the houses were just different dabs of pink, yellow, and blue — like flowers.

Julia almost reached out to touch the initials in the lower right corner. P.S., she read. Funny, the first thing Julia thought of was the word *postscript*. Like an extra message.

"P.S.?" she asked Mrs. Bowen.

"Penelope Sauri," Edna explained. "That was her maiden name before she married Ulysses Moore. She was Italian."

An idea suddenly struck Julia. "May I?" she asked. Julia gently lifted the frame off the wall.

She turned it over, hoping to find some writing — some kind of clue — on the back of the canvas. She found something else. A small object was attached by Scotch tape. Julia carefully peeled it off.

The others drew close. "What did you find, Julia?" Rick asked.

Julia turned it over in her hand, puzzled.

"What is it, dear?" asked Edna. She took a towel and wiped the object clean.

It was less than a finger high, tapered gently, and had a sort of crown at the top. The bottom was covered with green velvet.

"It's some kind of weird chess piece," Rick concluded. "A pawn, I think. But not from an ordinary set."

"No," Julia said. "It's a queen. I'm sure of it."

Jason scratched his nose, thoughtfully. "Okay, let's summarize. Here's a queen . . . that was hidden behind the canvas of a painting . . . which was given by Penelope Moore . . . as a thank-you gift . . . for the

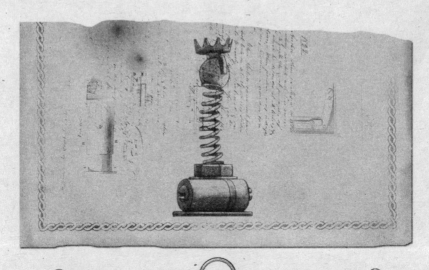

surgery performed by Dr. Bowen . . . on the lighthouse keeper . . . who was bitten by a shark!"

"That's about it," Rick said.

"Sure, easy," Julia said. "Or as Sherlock Holmes might say, 'Elementary, my dear Watson!'"

"But where does it all lead us?" Jason asked, bewildered.

"To town," Julia replied. She turned to Edna and winked. "I simply must do something with my hair!"

With the Bowens' approval, Jason pocketed the chess piece. His heart began to soar with hope.

But that was before he saw the bike.

- Chapter 7 -
A QUESTION OF LOOKS

Hurry up, will you?" Julia shouted at her brother. "There's nobody looking!"

Jason scowled and reluctantly mounted the bike. It had once been owned by the Bowens' daughter — not that anyone could tell from looking at it. The bike was a brilliant fuchsia pink and featured butterfly-shaped handlebars complete with multicolored streamers and a little white basket.

As soon as they reached the first building in Kilmore Cove, Jason dismounted. "We're here," he announced. "I'm walking the rest of the way."

Julia found this hysterical.

"Give me a break," Jason complained. "I can't be seen on a girl's bike! I've got a reputation to protect. Why don't we switch?"

Julia just grinned, thoroughly enjoying Jason's predicament. "You're the one who destroyed the other bike. You're lucky to have a bike at all. Isn't that right, Rick?"

The redheaded boy snickered. He agreed whole-heartedly. "Traitors," Jason muttered darkly.

They passed a group of fishermen who were sitting on an old bench, talking about this and that. Pushing the girl's bicycle, Jason tried to walk in front of the men with dignity, but it was hard not to think that all the chuckling that followed was aimed at him.

Guided by Rick, the twins left the sea behind them and proceeded onto a narrow lane that brought them to the center of town. The pavement beneath their feet was an old-fashioned flagstone. The colorful window frames, painted in yellows and blues, added charm to the white houses whose small terraces brimmed with colorful flowers.

They passed a bakery that emitted an irresistible aroma. Julia felt herself filled with a sense of well-being. It really was a beautiful town. A special, magical place. Kilmore Cove. It was beginning to feel like home, even for a city girl like herself.

They passed by the vegetable stand and waved at the owner, who was sitting in front of the store, soaking up the sun. The woman returned Rick's greeting warmly and, in turn, waved at the girl and the boy with the funny pink bike.

The narrow street forked at the statue of King William V. It was a majestic monument depicting the sovereign sitting on a horse, galloping toward the sea. Jason and Julia, who had never seen it, found the statue captivating — and strangely familiar.

Rick wanted to cross the center of town as quickly as possible. He spurred them forward into a small square where outdoor tables were set neatly in front of a small restaurant. He stopped, looked around to get his bearings, and proceeded on.

"This is it," he told them. He stopped in front of a shop with two signs. The first one read: HIGH SOCIETY HAIR SALON. The one beside it read: SHAVE AND HAIRCUTS FOR MEN. There were two windows and two entrances, one below each sign.

"Which entrance should we use?" Jason wondered.

"I'm going to try the High Society Hair Salon," Julia announced. "I sure didn't come here for a shave." She parted the plastic curtain of dangling beads and entered.

"I guess I'll try the other door," Rick decided.

Jason, still in a sour mood, stayed outside with the bikes.

Gwendaline jumped up from her seat as soon as Julia set foot inside the salon. "Hey there!" she said warmly, with a kind smile. She was a young woman, very thin, with a bright, sunny smile and owlish, round eyes. Wild black hair framed her face's sharp, dramatic features.

"Please come in," Gwendaline said, gesturing to a chair in front of a mirror. She held up a finger, listening intently. "Ah, when it rains, it pours. Please excuse me for a moment."

The hair stylist walked through a narrow opening in the wall and appeared in front of Rick.

"Hello," Gwendaline said. She stared at Rick for

a moment, and said, "Don't tell me, don't tell me. You are . . . you are . . . I know I've seen you before . . . and your name is . . ."

"Rick Banner," Rick finally replied.

"I knew it!" Gwendaline exclaimed triumphantly. "You have your mother's hair and eyes." She paused, smiling kindly. "Please have a seat. I have a client on the other side."

Rick told her that they had come together.

Gwendaline raised an eyebrow, as if this was indeed significant information. "Your girlfriend, is she?" she asked. "Ah, to be young and foolish. I envy you two lovebirds!"

Gwendaline ignored Rick's pointed protests. She merely smiled and replied, "Ah, but a woman knows."

Rick followed her into the High Society Hair Salon. Which was, of course, really the same building, divided in half.

"I don't understand," Rick said. "Why two shops?"

Gwendaline laughed. "It's simple: Women don't like being seen by men with curlers on their heads, and men don't like to be seen being shaved by a ladies' hairdresser."

"It makes sense to me," Julia agreed. "That's very smart of you." She liked Gwendaline immediately.

And Julia suspected that most people, both men and women, did as well. To be a true town gossip, people must feel at ease around you. Otherwise, they would never confide their secrets.

Gwendaline picked up a pair of scissors. "Who shall I begin with?" she asked.

"Actually, um . . ."

The hairdresser suddenly pointed at Julia. "That accent. You're from London, aren't you?" Her round eyes widened in recognition. "Of course! Silly me! You must be one of the twins who moved into the old Moore place."

"Julia Covenant," Julia replied, extending her hand. "I'm pleased to meet you."

While they shook hands, Gwendaline winked conspiratorially at Rick, as if to say, *Isn't she the nice catch!*

"It's not that way," Rick protested. "We're just friends."

Gwendaline smiled and raised both eyebrows. "Maybe you are more than that," she said, "but you don't know it yet."

Rick looked uncomfortably toward the front door. Maybe it wasn't too late to escape.

"And your brother?" Gwendaline asked Julia. "Where is he today?"

"Right outside," Julia said.

Gwendaline quickly moved to the front window. She parted the curtains, knocked on the glass, and motioned for Jason to come in. It was an offer that Jason couldn't refuse.

Before Jason realized what hit him, he found himself seated on a chair with a warm towel wrapped around his neck and Gwendaline's scissors dancing around his head. It was, he thought, very relaxing. Gwendaline had a way of making people feel good.

Fifteen minutes later, Jason was admiring his new hipster haircut in the mirror. His hair was twisted into place and hardened by gel. "I'm totally rocking now," he noted with satisfaction.

On the way out, Julia asked the question they had come to get answered. "Oblivia Newton?" Gwendaline asked. "Yes, I know her. She's one of my clients."

"Can you tell us where she lives?" Julia asked, trying to sound innocent.

"Certainly," Gwendaline answered. "Are you on foot?"

"Bikes," Rick answered.

"Even better," Gwendaline said, "because it's a bit of a hike. You need to take the coastal road after

the pier. Or I suppose you could go back up and make a turn in front of Calypso's Island."

Rick groaned. "We better not. I think we should avoid Ms. Calypso's bookstore for the time being."

That raised Gwendaline's gossip antenna. "And tell me, why on earth should you avoid such an interesting woman?"

"We promised that we'd read some books," Rick explained, "and we've been kind of busy with other stuff."

"Yeah, kind of," Julia joked.

The hairdresser eyed Julia closely, almost suspiciously. Then she turned back to Rick. "Well, you can always go to the square with the king's statue. You'll come out by the boardwalk. Then take a right. Just remember to always keep the sea on your left. Keep going for several miles and you'll come to the grooved road at Owl Clock. Continue for about two more miles, and you'll find yourself in a small grove of exotic trees. Oblivia told me," Gwendaline confided, "she had them imported from far away. She has a beautiful house, very modern. It looks like a purple upside-down chiffon cake. Seriously! You can't miss it!"

The three friends thanked her and headed off toward town. Jason was so excited about his new look that he completely forgot that he was riding such a ridiculous bicycle. He took off at breakneck speed, eager to get to Oblivia's house.

They raced past the king's statue and took a right in an alley so narrow that the roofs of the houses almost touched one another. Arriving at an opening where the old stone houses aligned in a neat row like soldiers, they saw an old woman dressed in only a bathrobe. She was standing in the middle of the street, waving her arms frantically. "Slow down!" she screamed, extremely agitated. "You'll run over Marcus Aurelius!"

"Miss Biggles!" Rick exclaimed. He leaped off his bike. "What happened? Are you all right?"

Miss Biggles, still wearing her nightgown and slippers, had been roaming the street in a state of confusion. Her hair was disheveled. She was beside herself with worry. Rick talked to her soothingly and tried to get her to calm down, but the frail old woman found it impossible to focus.

"Marcus Aurelius ran out!" she whimpered, covering her face with her hands. "He got frightened of those people and fled, I'm afraid."

Jason stole a look at Julia. "I guess the circus is in town," he quipped.

"Shush," Julia replied angrily. "Can't you ever be nice?"

After several unsuccessful attempts to explain what happened, Miss Biggles pointed to a cat perched on top of a street lamp on the opposite side of the street.

"There he is," she exclaimed. "My little Marcus! Look at him. He's completely terrorized!"

"Don't worry, Miss Biggles," Rick said, gently taking the frightened old woman by the arm. "You stay right here on the sidewalk. We'll take care of your cat."

Jason rolled his eyes impatiently. "Rick," he hissed, "we don't have time for this. It's a long ride to Oblivia Newton's and . . ."

Upon hearing that name, Miss Biggles grew more agitated. She turned to Jason with a wild look in her eyes. "Ms. Newton?! You're going to see Ms. Newton?"

"Yes," Julia answered.

"I know her!" Miss Biggles cried. "I know her all too well." She put her hands on her ears and squeezed her eyes shut. Gesturing wildly with her hands, Miss Biggles hurried toward her house. At the door-step, she turned and shouted, "It's all her fault, you know. Marcus Aurelius and my sweethearts were so frightened. All her fault — and that nasty dripping brute of a man!"

She opened the door, and a dozen mewling cats scampered out. They curled around her feet, crying for her attention.

"Behave, my darlings," Miss Biggles said in admonishment. "Marcus Aurelius will be back soon. The sweet children have come to help us."

Easier said than done, Rick thought to himself as he struggled to shimmy up the lamppost. The cat, curled up on the curve of the pole, was looking at Rick with extreme interest. No matter how many sweet words or stern commands the kids tried, they could not convince him to come down.

Finally, Jason lost his patience. Sweet talk wasn't working. So he walked up to the lamppost and gave it a thunderous kick. Frightened by the noise, Marcus Aurelius leaped to the ground, hissing. A second later, he sprinted toward the house and hid between Miss Biggles' legs.

"Marcus Aurelius," the old woman cried in relief. "You've come back!"

Jason smiled with satisfaction. "Mission accomplished," he said. "Now let's ride."

But Rick and Julia were too well-mannered for such a hasty escape, tempting as it was. They were still concerned about Miss Biggles, who truly seemed distraught and unbalanced.

Miss Biggles, for her part, insisted on thanking the "dear children" by offering cookies. Despite Jason's desperate protests, she would not take no for an answer.

"Come into my kitchen!" she said, showing them into her house. "I can't eat them all myself, you know, otherwise I'd grow to look like an old cow."

Julia, curious as ever, quickly followed Miss Biggles into the house. There was something mysterious going on — the woman seemed to grow upset at the mere mention of Oblivia's name — and Julia was eager to discover why. Rick followed, urging a grumpy Jason along. "A few cookies will do us good," Rick reasoned.

Once they were inside the house, however, Jason's mood quickly changed. As he passed through the entrance hall, he felt a gritty texture beneath his feet. Jason stopped and knelt down, touching the floor with his fingers. Sand. Grains of sand. But how? From where?

He looked up at the wall. But it was not a wall. It was . . . a door. The sand seemed to come from the other side.

Meanwhile, Miss Cleopatra Biggles rattled plates in the kitchen, talking incessantly about cats and cookies and a soggy, mule-faced man.

Jason touched his gelled hair. He touched the thin layer of sand that covered the floor. Tiny grains stuck to his fingers. They were exactly like those he'd found in the stone room in Argo Manor.

It was the same fine sand.

Desert sand.

And it seemed to come from beneath that door.

His mind raced in a thousand directions. Oblivia Newton had been here. Yes, that's what the crazy old woman had said. Oblivia scared the cat. And . . . and . . . the mule-faced man? That was Manfred, it had to be. Oblivia had traveled in time, just as they had. Could it be possible that there was another door?

This door.

"Julia, Rick," Jason said in a hoarse whisper. "You've got to see this."

The hall door, which he now carefully examined, looked ancient. It was sturdy, thick, made of dark wood. In fact, it was the same color as the door at Argo Manor. The exact same color.

Jason tried to open the door.

It was locked.

"Miss Biggles," Jason asked politely. "Can you open this door?"

Miss Biggles came into the passageway holding a plate of cookies. She said that she couldn't

remember it ever being opened. There were no keys to it. She thought of it, she told Jason, as if it were a wall. "Doors lead to places, don't they?" she said. "This one does not even open. It's just a fancy wall."

Jason showed her the sand between his fingers.

"Probably from the cats," Miss Biggles explained. She bit into a butter cookie, munching contentedly.

Julia and Rick stood beside Jason, their eyes fixed on the door. It was strikingly similar to the door at Argo Manor, yet also different. Smaller somehow. Somehow less . . . important. But the old nails on the left side of the massive lock were exactly like those on the door in Argo Manor.

Rick graciously accepted a cookie from Miss Biggles. They took a seat in what she called her sitting room, like it was a regular tea party. Rick cautiously brought up the subject: "Miss Biggles, do you think you could tell us what happened yesterday?"

The old lady tried to explain it, but her mind seemed cloudy, as if the actual facts were swimming in a fog. She mentioned Oblivia Newton, of course, and the bizarre visit in the middle of the night. There was a storm. The cats were restless. The large man frightened them. "Cats know these things," Miss Biggles explained. "They know about people. Instinct, you know. And they did not like that man. No, not at all."

"Anything else?" Rick asked.

Miss Biggles strained to remember, but finally gave a helpless shrug. "Nothing," she said. "Just a deep sleep. I awoke with a terrible headache."

It was late when she woke up, Miss Biggles explained. The cats were pacing, uneasy.

"Miss Biggles," Julia said gently, "can you think of any reason why those two came to your house in the middle of the night?"

Miss Biggles fingered the buttons on her night-gown. "Ms. Newton has always been unpredictable."

"So, you've known her for a long time?" Rick asked.

"Oh yes! Many years. Though I must confess, I never liked her," Miss Biggles said, glancing heaven-ward as if to ask for forgiveness. "Ms. Newton was a friend of my sister's."

"Your sister?" Julia repeated.

"Oblivia was once her favorite student," Miss Biggles explained.

"Student?" Jason said, now utterly confused. "Miss Biggles, please, what in the world are you talking about?"

Cleopatra Biggles reached down to pet one of her cats, and somehow that simple act seemed to settle her, calm her mind. She looked at Jason thoughtfully, remembering. "Oblivia Newton was a student at the

Cheddar Elementary School. Cheddar, of course, is the town where they make cheddar cheese."

"Fascinating," Jason groaned.

Julia kicked him in the shin.

Miss Biggles reached for a framed photo. It showed an old black-and-white photo of two girls sitting next to each other, arm in arm.

"I am the youngest," pointed out Miss Biggles. "This one is my sister, Nessa. To be precise, Clitemnestra Biggles. She was the brains in our family, even if our parents wanted both of us to have a career. Nessa loved to read. Oh, did she ever. Nessa gave me all the books you see in this room. She loved travel, adventure, and longed to see the world! And so," Miss Biggles continued, "when she came of age, Nessa left Kilmore Cove to teach at Cheddar. Oblivia Newton was a very smart and promising young student. That's how they came to know each other."

"What happened next?" Julia prompted.

"The years passed. My sister eventually returned to Kilmore Cove. She lived here with me, two old spinsters no longer alone. A few years ago, Nessa recognized a photo in the newspaper of the girl she knew in Cheddar. The student had grown to become a successful businesswoman. Nessa was thrilled, so proud, the way all teachers are proud of their success stories. So Nessa contacted her, I suppose. A card or a phone call, I do not know. Oblivia Newton came here, into our house. And she still returns from time to time, often without notice. It's strange," Cleopatra Biggles said thoughtfully. "She still visits, even though my sister died two years ago."

Throughout this story, Jason remained mostly silent. He could not keep from looking at the door in the hall. His heart was beating wildly. His hands were warm, sweaty. He was thrilled, of course, but also oddly disappointed. So there was another door. That made the door at Argo Manor — his door — not quite as special. It was no longer the only one.

While Miss Biggles went off to feed the cats, Jason talked it over with Rick and Julia in furtive whispers.

"How can we open it?" he wondered.

"Do you think this door also leads to a grotto? And to a ship like the one in Salton Cliff?" Julia asked.

"Yes," Jason nodded. "I do."

"Freaky deaky," Julia said.

"It explains how Oblivia got to ancient Egypt," Rick reasoned.

Julia reached into her pocket. She drew out the

keys to the door at Argo Manor. Owl, porcupine, elephant, newt.

"Should I?" she asked.

Each of the four keys fit into the lock. All four turned. But nothing happened. The door remained shut.

"None of them work!" Jason said, disappointed.

"They aren't the right ones," Jason said. "These keys open the door inside Argo Manor. This one must need a different key. . . ."

"And," Julia said, "Oblivia Newton probably has it."

Everything seemed to be coming together.

"We have to find her," Jason said with conviction. "She must have returned from Egypt by now."

"We don't know that," Rick said.

"Come on, Rick," Jason responded. "She got the map. She took it from us. It's a map of Kilmore Cove! The map once belonged to the Moores. The Moores took it to Egypt — hiding it like a needle in a haystack."

Rick gritted his teeth. "Yes, and she used us to find it."

"Exactly," Jason said. "It's not about Egypt — that was just a hiding place."

"A hiding place?!" Julia scoffed. "What's with

these people? Couldn't they just hide it under a bed or, I don't know, in a closet or something? Oh no. That would be too easy. They've got to go all the way to Egypt! What a bunch of wackos!"

"Now you are the one who deserves a kick in the shin," Jason scolded Julia. "This is serious stuff. It's, like, sacred even. We can't joke around."

"Whatever you say," Julia moaned.

"The map is of Kilmore Cove," Rick said, trying to think it through. "We know there are two doors. Do you understand?! Two magical doors . . . in the same old town, my hometown. What is going on around here?" Rick left the rest of his thoughts unspoken. But a shiver crawled up his spine.

"Could there be a third door?" Julia asked.

Jason looked at Rick. "Yeah, I guess there could be."

"Then maybe that explains the map," Rick said.

"Okaaay," Julia said. "Like, um, how?"

"The map is old, right?" Rick said, his voice growing intense.

"The date on it read: *One thousand seven hundred and something*," Jason remembered.

"Old town, old doors, old map," Rick said. "Maybe, just maybe, the map and the doors are connected."

"Makes sense," Julia admitted. "Sure."

"Would you like cups of tea, children?" Miss Biggles asked, sticking her head through a crack in the kitchen door.

Ten minutes later, Rick, Jason, and Julia were on their way to Oblivia Newton's once more.

"I burned my mouth on that tea!" Jason complained.

"You didn't have to drink it that fast," Julia said.

"I wanted to get out of there so bad," Jason answered. "I just poured it down my throat. Ouch!"

Rick and Julia laughed. They were reenergized, light-headed, giddy.

Before leaving, they had been able to convince Miss Biggles to place a heavy trunk in front of the hall door, blocking it from being opened.

"I don't understand," Miss Biggles protested.

"Just . . . just . . . please," Jason said. "Leave the trunk here."

"I can hardly move it without you," Miss Biggles complained. "It's far too heavy for me."

"And don't speak to anyone, okay?" Rick warned her for the second time. "You have to be careful, Miss Biggles."

"I still don't understand," she said, shaking her head in bewilderment.

"For the cats," Jason said. "Think of poor Marcus whatever-his-name-is, scared to death up there on that pole. We don't want that to happen again, do we, Miss Biggles?"

Miss Biggles nodded, an endless series of little head bobs, like nervous shaking. "Poor Marcus Aurelius," she murmured.

With the children gone, Cleopatra Biggles cleaned out the teacups. She put the cookies away. And she climbed the stairs to her bedroom. She thought about the lovely children who had visited. Such imaginations! *Ah, to be young*, Miss Biggles thought enviously. *Such a wonderful thing, to be young and happy.*

Jason and the girl, Julia, must be brother and sister, Miss Biggles decided. *And Rick Banner has always been such a good boy. Very kind. So sad about his father. He died so young.* Then she paused, wondering: *Whatever happened to the other Banner boy?* She sat on her bed, puzzled. *There were two Banners. Two sons. Strange . . .*

The old woman went into the bathroom, conversing with her cats Nero and Caracallus. She raised her head, looked at the mirror, and grimaced. Such an old face in the mirror. Who could that be? Could it really be her? Could the years have flown by so quickly? She tried distractedly to comb her hair.

But her arms were thin and weak. Little things took so much strength from her.

She left the brush hanging in her tangled hair. Even so, Cleopatra Biggles was unusually happy. It was as if, after the shock and fear from the preceding night, the arrival of the children had put her at ease. Their gentleness, their innocence, made her feel better.

And, yes, she had to confess, their sense of mystery was exciting — even for a used-up old woman. "'Now promise me you won't speak to anyone!'" Cleopatra Biggles said to herself, imitating Julia's concerned voice. That little girl was adorable. She reminded her of herself when she was that age.

"That's what I need!" Miss Biggles told her cats. "I will get dressed and go into town for one of Gwendaline's hairdos! She does a lovely job, and she always has gossip to share!"

As she was about to depart, the telephone rang. The sound startled her. It had been such a long time since it rang, Miss Biggles couldn't quite remember where she kept it.

"I'm coming! I'm coming!" she called to the old-fashioned telephone. She finally located it on a counter in the kitchen.

"Hello. Who's speaking?"

Cleopatra Biggles furrowed her forehead, worried and uncertain, before her face relaxed into a smile. "Nestor! Of course I remember you!" she exclaimed. "It's so nice to hear your voice. It has been a long, long time."

- Chapter 8 -
ON THE ROAD

WILLIAM V
SQUARE

Jason, Julia, and Rick pedaled along the quiet coastal road of Kilmore Cove. The road hugged the bay and wound around to the opposite side of Salton Cliff. They rode slowly, three across, in no hurry. The day was exquisite, as days often are after a great storm. The sky was clear, the sun a dandelion yellow.

Jason rode in the middle, between Julia and Rick. He could feel the weight of the metal chess piece that his sister had found behind Penelope Moore's painting in his pocket.

Julia was driving him crazy with all her questions. That was how she thought about things, Jason realized. She asked questions, one after another after another. In seeking the answer, that was how she came to an understanding. It worked! But as far as Jason was concerned, it was still annoying. But then, he thought, sisters often are. And all things considered, Julia wasn't half-bad. He'd seen worse.

But still: Julia asked about Penelope, Ulysses, Dr. Bowen, Oblivia, the lighthouse keeper — "We hardly know *anything* about him!" Julia exclaimed. "Bitten by a shark? What's that all about?!"

Every new piece in the puzzle had to be examined, mulled over, debated. Each time they pieced something together, the entire puzzle seemed to take on a new shape, forcing them to consider new possibilities, to arrange the puzzle in a completely new way. It was exhausting.

The twins felt as if they had lived in Kilmore Cove all their lives, not just a few days. Less than twenty-four hours ago they had deciphered the first secret message. A message that someone had put into code, seemingly just for them. That's what Jason thought, anyway. He was convinced that someone had purposely set a hard course for them to follow. That Sunday, however, it had gotten more complicated. The clues were clouded, obscure. They could stare at a code and try to figure it out. But now it had changed. They lacked answers. They were still trying to learn the right questions.

"If there's another Door to Time, and Oblivia knows all about it," Rick said, "why is she so hot to get to the one in Argo Manor?"

"It must be different somehow," Julia said.

"I agree," Rick replied.

"But both doors lead to Egypt," Jason pointed out. "Explain that."

"The door didn't lead to Egypt," Rick replied. "Or don't you remember, Captain Jason? You were the one who brought us to Egypt. It was you."

Jason shook his head. "But it wasn't my idea," he

countered. "I just followed the clues in the journal. I'm not leading us anywhere. I'm following a trail that was laid for us, like Hansel and Gretel's bread crumbs in the dark forest."

"Ugh." Julia sighed. "I'm so confused!"

"Well, let's think small," Rick suggested. "We are on the road, heading to Oblivia Newton's house. Maybe that's enough for now."

"Nestor said it a couple of times," Julia reminded them. "He keeps saying that she was 'a terrible mistake.'"

"Maybe, just maybe, it was Nessa Biggles who committed the terrible mistake," offered Jason.

Rick shook his head. "Maybe, but that's just guess-work. We need facts. Proof. Right now, we still have no clue what's really in her mind, and that, guys, is the real problem."

"I think that the real mystery is Kilmore Cove," said Jason. "At first I thought it was just Argo Manor, but now after seeing Miss Biggles' door, and thinking about that map, I'm starting to think that this whole town is —"

"— right out of the Twilight Zone," Julia interrupted. "Weirdsville, England."

"My guess," Jason continued, glancing toward Rick, "is that someone wants to keep these doors a secret. The door in Argo Manor was hidden behind a huge armoire. If we hadn't found it by mistake, it would have stayed hidden for years. Miss Biggles, well, she has absolutely no *idea* what's going on!"

Julia laughed. "No, but those were some pretty terrific cookies, I'll give her that."

"We need to open her door," Jason said.

"Yeah, okaaay," Julia said in exasperation. "How are we going to manage that trick, Jason? Our keys don't work!"

"Don't get snippy with me," Jason shot back. "Maybe the one you threw in the sea last night would have opened it," he grumbled.

"What?!" Julia screamed. "Jason, do me a favor and shut up. You weren't there. You have no idea what you're talking about. He was trying to kill me."

Rick pulled his bike to a halt. "Guys, stop it already. You fight like cats and dogs."

"Or like brothers and sisters," Julia and Jason said at the same time. Then they both laughed. Twins. They often said and thought the same things at exactly the same moment. They were linked. And no matter how badly they fought, it never changed their fundamental relationship. They were truly two peas in a pod, connected in deep ways.

"Look where we are," Rick said, waving his hand

across the horizon. They had arrived at a point on the road where the coast forked. On their right, the road continued, while on the left, a narrow spit of land stretched out into the water, like a finger pointing. At the end was the lighthouse, alone in the distance — almost as if it were sitting atop the water itself.

Julia scanned the white rocks of Salton Cliff on the opposite side of the bay. Argo Manor, whose tower rose above the tops of trees, sat high upon the cliff. An amazing house. The cliffside staircase leading down to the beach was carved into the rock. From across the bay, at this distance, it looked like it was cut into two pieces. The jagged edges reminded Julia of the teeth of a great white shark.

"Should we have told Nestor?" she asked, a trace of concern in her voice. "He might worry."

"Nestor? Worry?" scoffed Jason. "I doubt it. He cares more about his gardenias than us."

"I disagree," Julia said. "Anyway, maybe we could call him."

"Look around, Julia," Jason said. "Do you see any phone booths? We're pedaling into the middle of nowhere. There's no turning back now."

"Really, Julia," Rick said, not unkindly. "I know you're thinking about him, but don't worry. Nestor is probably raking leaves, making soup, puttering around the grounds doing his usual stuff. I just don't see him as a worrier."

"Exactly my point," Julia replied. "We should be the ones worrying about him. He's an old man. He's sick. He might need our help."

"Dr. Bowen said he's as hard as a rock," Jason said.

"True," Julia replied. "But don't forget, he's the only person who knows about our secret. If we need a friend in Kilmore Cove, he's all we've got."

"Oh, I didn't realize that you two had gotten so buddy-buddy," Jason said.

"Yeah, he's my new boyfriend — I'm dating gee-zers now," Julia joked. Then she shook her head. "Let's just go."

Jason grabbed Julia's handlebars. "Hey," he said. "Let's not fight. We're a team, Julia. I need you."

His eyes looked into hers — twinned eyes, locked together. He was sincere, genuine. "I know," Julia said. "I'm just worried about him. It's a feeling. I can't explain it."

"What feeling?" Rick asked.

Julia looked across the water to the house upon the cliff. "I just feel like something is going to happen."

"Like what?" Rick prodded.

"I don't know," Julia answered. "Something bad."

- Chapter 9 -
SPINNING

Inside a purple house, just two miles from where Julia, Rick, and Jason had stopped, a telephone rang. It rang, and rang, and rang.

A woman pedaled on a sophisticated exercise bicycle designed for "spinning" sessions — the very latest fitness trend. Loud music throbbed until the paint threatened to peel from the walls. Lights flashed, on and off. And the woman on the bike, staring straight ahead as if in a trance, pedaled faster and faster. She dripped with sweat until every muscle burned, until her lungs were on fire. And still she pedaled harder, faster, more and more. Burning, burning, burning.

After about the twentieth ring, a white door swung open into the room. The music stopped. The bicycle slowed to a halt.

"Manfred," the woman said. "I said I was not to be disturbed."

"I'm sorry, Ms. Newton," her beefy assistant groveled. "There's a phone call."

"This had better be good," Oblivia said, her face red and flushed with sweat.

"It's the guy from the construction crew," Manfred said.

Oblivia's eyes widened. "Send it through to my private line," she ordered.

Manfred nodded. He did not say that that was exactly what he had been trying to do for the past few minutes. He knew better than that. Manfred merely nodded, bit his tongue, and followed orders. It was how he earned a living, doing as he was told. Some days, he reflected, it was awfully hard work.

Oblivia Newton dried herself with a dark purple towel, monogrammed with her initials: *O.N.* This time, she answered the phone on the first ring. "Speak," she barked into the receiver. Oblivia listened for a few moments, then impatiently cut the caller off in midsentence. "Cost is not an issue, have I not already made that clear? The job must be done today, immediately. I don't want excuses. Or stories. Or reasons why you can't. You either do the job on my terms, for a handsome fee, or I will hire someone else. End of story." She paused, closing her eyes. "I don't care if there isn't a wall left standing by the time you are done. Just find that door, even if you have to take that house apart piece by piece."

On the other end of the telephone, the foreman of the construction crew nodded, interjecting the words, "Yes, Ms. Newton," every few moments. It was a job. A crazy job for an insane, irritating woman. But she was also extremely wealthy. She paid well. So if she wanted to turn a perfectly good house into a pile

of rubble, who was he to argue? Just so long as the check didn't bounce.

Before hanging up, however, he did have to ask one final question. Directions.

Oblivia sighed, bored with the tedious details. "Take the small grooved path leading out of town. You can't miss it. No, no, I don't care if you need a permit. The house is mine, and I'll do whatever I want with it! This job goes under the radar, do you understand? No permits, no government agencies snooping around. That's why you get paid so well. Am I clear? Good, very good. I'll see you in twenty minutes."

She hung up the receiver and smiled. A perfect smile. Full red lips, straight white teeth, and all the wickedness of the world in her icy blue eyes.

Oblivia tossed the towel on the floor. A servant would pick it up later. She left the room, shouting as she pushed open the door. "Manfred, we're leaving in fifteen minutes."

He had been standing in silence, hands in his pockets, staring through a large window. He turned stiffly, as if his body was sore — as if the effort gave him pain. His nose was bandaged, his face puffy and swollen. He had a weary look, with dark circles around his eyes, as if he had been in a fight the previous night — and lost, badly.

"Where are we going?" he asked.

Oblivia Newton stopped, surprised at such an impertinent question. "When it's your business, I'll let you know," she sneered.

"Ms. Newton," Manfred said, taking a half step forward. He took his hands out of his pockets and lifted them, palms out. His words were soft, almost pleading, "I did it for you."

Oblivia dug her nails into the palms of her hands. She clenched them into fists, enjoying the small shock of pain it brought her.

"Save your apologies, Manfred," Oblivia said flatly. "You know how angry I was when I returned to that hideous home for wayward cats and found you missing, against my orders. No, you decided to take a little joyride to Argo Manor." She paused, eyes narrowing. "Tell me, Manfred. Whatever did become of my car?"

Manfred's face turned pale. He lowered his head, eyes on the ground.

"However, all is forgiven," Oblivia said in a sing-songy voice, changing moods in a flash. "You provided me with such a beautiful stolen object . . . that I have decided to forgive you." She walked up to him and touched him, once, gently, on the face.

Manfred felt off-balance, uncertain.

Two old keys flashed in Oblivia's hand.

"I only had the cat," she purred, fingering one key. "And it was so lonely. But you, Manfred, have given me the lion."

Manfred swallowed, both frightened and secretly thrilled at being so close to his employer.

Oblivia turned away, breaking the spell. "I'm going to shower and change. We must hurry, Manfred, for today is a momentous day. Get the motorcycle ready. We'll be leaving shortly."

The man watched her until Oblivia had disappeared into the upstairs bedroom. He thrust his meaty hands back into his pockets. He felt himself boil with anger, rage, passion. He wanted to punch something, anything, before he exploded. He hated his job. He hated Argo Manor. He hated the old caretaker. He hated that girl who had nearly killed him. Hate was the fuel that fed him, the fuel that burned inside him, day after day. He realized, with shock, that he was beginning to hate his boss as well. The Queen of Thieves. Beautiful, powerful, and alluring. She used him and abused him. And yet, for one kind word, one soft touch . . .

He would do anything for her approval.

Anything at all.

- Chapter 10 -
OWL CLOCK

The kids stopped to rest at a crossing by a narrow grooved road. Since leaving town, they had not seen a single car. The landscape had changed into a flat expanse of low-lying bushes, stunted by the harsh salt air, and of white and purple flowers that dotted the horizon. Every so often a lone tree, with branches curved inland by the steady sea breeze, stood out like a sentry.

Rick, who always thought ahead, had filled a large canteen with water. He now shared it with the twins, who drank from it gratefully.

The grooved road looked as if it had been recently trampled by a big piece of machinery. It had left deep tracks in the dirt. The street sign had been knocked down. Jason picked it up. "*Owl Clock*," he read aloud. "Weird name for a road, don't you think?"

Julia remembered what Dr. Bowen had said earlier. She asked Rick, "Is it true that you've never seen a sign that says, WELCOME TO KILMORE COVE? I thought there were signs like that at the border of every town?"

Rick screwed the top back on the canteen. "Truthfully, I never paid attention to it. But now that I think about it, yeah, I don't think there're any signs."

"How many roads lead to town?" Julia asked.

"This is it," Rick said. "As you can see, it's not exactly bustling with traffic."

Julia looked down the quiet road. "Nope, this sure isn't Piccadilly Circus."

"I wouldn't know," Rick said to Julia. "The truth is, I've never been outside of Kilmore Cove."

"Get out!" Julia exclaimed, shocked.

"For real," Rick said, laughing at Julia's reaction.

"Never? Never *ever*?" Julia asked.

"I love it here," Rick told her. "I just never saw a reason to leave."

Julia noticed Rick's embarrassment. She was beginning to enjoy his gentleness and simplicity. He was so different from all the other boys she knew.

Jason joined the conversation. "Is there a train station around here?" he wondered.

"Used to be," Rick replied. "But it's been closed for years. I guess we're a little out of the way."

"I'll say!" Jason agreed.

"But you know what?" Rick said, a little defensively. "We like it that way. The people here in Kilmore Cove, it's like we don't need the rest of the world. It can go on spinning without us, because we've got everything we need right here." He looked at Julia. "Does that make any sense?"

Julia nodded, "Yeah, I think so — in a bizarre, freaky kind of way."

"Maybe it makes you uncomfortable," Rick suggested. "Being out here in the middle of nowhere."

Julia didn't answer. She just shut her eyes and let the silence wrap around her. *No,* she thought. *It feels nice. Peaceful.*

They remained silent for a few moments. Finally Rick said, "Well, I love it here. Even if there are no signs that say WELCOME TO KILMORE COVE! And, um," he hesitated, "I'm really glad you guys are here, too."

"Oh great," Jason groaned. "Now I want to hurl. Let's get going before this conversation gets any mushier."

Rick's face flushed red. He pushed off the ground with his foot, hard, and raced ahead. *Stupid, stupid, stupid,* Rick chastised himself. *I made myself look like an idiot. She must really think I'm a country bumpkin. What's gotten into me? Why do I feel this way?* he wondered.

Rick thought of his father. He was a man of the world, a traveler, an adventurer. He knew exactly what to do and what to say. But for Rick, it wasn't so easy. How he wished, at times like these, that his father was still alive.

The loud roar of an engine broke the silence. It was growing louder, coming closer. It was a black motorcycle, traveling at a dangerous speed, hugging the curve like a panther.

"Look out, Rick!" Jason screamed in warning.

Rick had no time to react. The motorcycle was upon him in an instant. Instinctively, he threw himself to the left and fell to the ground. The motorcycle passed on his right, just inches away. It had two passengers.

Rick recognized them both.

The motorcycle did not stop. But it slowed when it reached the grooved road, turning inland.

Julia reached Rick first. "Wow, you almost got killed. Are you okay?"

"Yeah, yeah," Rick answered angrily. "I'm fine."

"It was them!" Jason said, bringing his bike to a skidding stop. "It was Manfred and Oblivia — I'm sure of it!"

"I know," Rick said. "That's the second time they've forced me off the road. And I'm getting pretty tired of it."

Julia looked down the road, where a cloud of dust had formed in the motorcycle's wake. "Where do you think they were headed?"

Rick jumped back on his bike. "They took that grooved road," he growled. "I'm going to follow them. I want to get those guys!"

"What are you gonna do?" Jason called after him.

"You'll see," Rick answered. Then he stood on his pedals and raced off, hungry for revenge.

"Let me understand you," said one of three fishermen to the lighthouse keeper. "You're willing to pay us a full week's wages just to throw the nets under the cliff?"

His two comrades scratched their beards, amused by the prospect of making so much money by fulfilling such an eccentric request.

"Leonard, I've known you a long time," the fisherman said. "So I've got to ask: Have you gone out of your mind?"

Great bursts of laughter erupted from the three fisherman.

The lighthouse keeper, Leonard Minaxo, smiled at the friendly joke. The fishermen did not understand, nor did he want them to understand. So he pulled himself to full height, sucked on his pipe, and waited for the laughter to subside. Leonard was a large man and well-respected for his prodigious strength. The laughter would not last.

"Mad or not," he finally addressed the gathered fishermen, "that is exactly my offer to you. Take it or leave it."

One of the fishermen — a thin, wiry fellow with a hooked nose — remarked, "If we cast the nets under the cliffs, like you ask, we'll just dredge the bottom. We won't catch any fish at all!"

His friend — older, plumper, and wiser — sagely commented, "But he isn't looking for fish — that's my bet. Am I right about that, Leonard?"

The lighthouse keeper shifted his weight from one foot to the other. He did not answer, but simply scowled at the question.

"I made my offer," he gruffly said. "It's a good amount of money. As for the rest — the whys and wherefores — I suggest you don't press the point."

"Sure, Leonard, we understand. It's your money and you're free to do whatever you want with it," the older fisherman said. "We'll cast the nets with weights and we'll see what we pull up. Fair enough?"

Leonard Minaxo pulled on his pipe and blew a ring of smoke into the air. It was a deal.

The old man could thank him later.

Alow cloud of dust from the motorcycle settled over Owl Clock's grooved road. The kids followed the bike's tracks easily, coughing often, as the unsettled dirt reached their lungs. The winding road sloped gently through green grass, thistles, and hardy yellow flowers. Before long, they arrived at the remains of an old gate, strangely out of place. It was made of two stone pillars now nearly overgrown with vines. Shards of mirror adorned the top of each column, remnants of an old decoration. The two halves of the rusted metal gate lay broken among the weeds, as if a large vehicle had crashed through them.

"Look at these tracks in the mud," Rick noted. "Somebody has come through here with some kind of tractor."

Julia read the old, battered brass plate that still hung on the gate:

MIRROR HOUSE

OWL CLOCK — KILMORE COVE

"Does that name ring a bell?" she asked Rick.

"Nope," he said. "But I guess we'll find out soon enough."

Beyond the gate, the path curved into a soft *s* between two grassy knolls. On top of one of the

hills, there was a row of strange-looking struc-
tures — tall, narrow windmills with long blades that
spun lazily in the afternoon breeze. The road was
flanked by trees thick with foliage, planted with
meticulous precision to create a perfect pathway.

"Do you hear that noise?" Jason asked the others.
"It sounds like . . . like . . ."

"A truck!" Rick screamed. "Get off the road, fast!"

A sturdy dump truck was headed their way, coming from the coastal road.

They quickly removed their bikes from the road
and hid behind the trees on the path, flattening themselves on the grass. The truck barreled past. Jason
peeked out to read the sign on the side of the truck:

DEMOLITION AND CONSTRUCTION
CYCLOPS & SONS

The truck went bouncing along, rumbling noisily, until it disappeared beyond the hill.

"We'd better be careful," whispered Jason. "Let's stay out of sight until we know what's going on."

The three kids hid the bikes with small branches and tufts of grass. Taking cover behind the trees, they followed the path up the hill. Once they reached the top, they caught sight of a bizarre house. Its roof seemed to be completely covered by mirrors. The house was tall and narrow, in keeping with the nearby windmills. Its walls were covered with ivy; the windows were adorned with ornamental wrought-iron railings.

As Rick, Jason, and Julia drew closer, they could see that the house had fallen into ill repair. It obviously had not been lived in for years. It was, Julia thought, like a great creature that had died, or was dying.

Standing in the front driveway was a group of thickly-muscled men and machinery. Off to the side of the road, the kids spied the motorcycle that had almost run over Rick. Beyond it was a large demolition crane with a long chain and an iron wrecking ball.

The men wore bright blue pants and, on their heads, bright blue caps sporting the emblem of an open eye. The Cyclops. The men were engaged in a conversation with Oblivia Newton. Manfred stood by her side. Oblivia was gesturing, pointing at the house, as if explaining what she wanted.

Jason shimmied through the grass, getting as close as possible. Rick and Julia followed his lead. As they inched closer, Julia had her first good look at Manfred. So he had survived after all. She felt relieved, and yet at the same time, she was filled with dread. Frightened, even.

"It looks like you broke his nose," Jason whispered, noticing Manfred's white bandage. "Serves him right."

"Wait for me here," Rick said, then scurried off through an opening in some bushes.

"But . . ."

"I'll be right back," he promised. "I have to do something."

"Do you need help?" Jason offered.

Rick grinned. "No, it's personal."

Jason and Julia crouched down on the grass, craning their necks to see.

"What's he going to do?" Julia whispered.

"He's angry," Jason replied. "That means he could do anything."

Julia coughed once, then covered her mouth with her hand.

Manfred looked around nervously, as if he had sensed the children nearby. Jason saw Rick disappear behind a dirt mound, then emerge a few moments later at the side of the huge truck. The twins anxiously followed their friend's movements as he crept closer to where Oblivia spoke with the men. Then Rick ducked in the other direction, using the truck to shield him from view. He was headed for the motorcycle.

"What are you up to now?" Julia whispered admiringly.

She watched as Rick bent down to the motorcycle's tires, made a quick movement, then disappeared into the thick brush.

"I think he slashed the tires," Jason said, eyes popping with delight. "I didn't know old Rick had it in him!"

Julia laughed soundlessly, secretly thrilled. Rick rejoined the twins a few minutes later. "Nice work," Jason whispered. Julia squeezed his hand.

"They deserve it," Rick observed, grinning slyly.

"Could you hear what they were talking about?" Julia asked.

"Not much," Rick admitted. "Oblivia was saying

that this house was her property. She sounds like a tough customer."

"We have to find out more," murmured Jason.

"How?" asked Julia anxiously. "It's too danger-ous to get as close as Rick did. If they catch us . . ."

"I found a dirt path," Rick said. "It's hidden by the bushes. It goes around to the back of the house, I think." He pointed at the brush alongside the back of the house. "Let's check it out. I think we can hide behind the house, and maybe hear better without being seen."

Jason nodded. "Lead the way, Lone Ranger."

As they circled around the back, hidden by the thicket of woods, Jason and Julia got their first close look at the house. It was like nothing they had ever seen before — a house built by a lunatic, or a mad scientist. For starters, the house seemed to have been built on top of a circular platform. The platform was set on iron pilings. All of this made the house appear as if it were resting on water. It looked more like a combination of steel, mirrors, ivy, and glass than an ordinary house.

Mesmerized, the children drew nearer. Several large birds had built their nests among the high-climbing vines and were curiously observing them, safely hidden in the shadows of the thick foliage. Rick

noted that the house and the circular platform were attached by massive iron bars and heavy bolts. Behind the ivy that covered the walls, metal cables and copper pipes ran the length of the house, forming a metal skeleton.

"It's brilliant," Rick said with awe, examining the bizarre construction. "Absolutely brilliant."

"Okaaay," Julia said. "Now do you want to explain why you think so?"

Rick put his head closer to Julia's. He pointed to various aspects of the house. "I believe that this platform," he explained, "is used to turn the house around. It revolves, like a merry-go-round!"

"Amazing," Julia whispered. "But why?"

"Why not?" Rick replied with a shrug. "Hey, I don't know! I mean, yeah, it's weird. But think about it, just from an engineering standpoint, it's staggering. Whoever built this house," Rick concluded, "was a genius."

"Maybe the mirrors on the roof are some kind of solar panels," Jason hypothesized. "And those windmills on top of the hill could all be a way to harness natural energy from the sun and the wind."

The low calling of a bird — *whoo, whoo* — floated down from the roof.

"Owls?" Rick asked, eyebrows raised.

Jason smiled. "I guess the sign didn't read 'Owl Clock' for nothing."

Even so, it became clear that they had failed in their main objective. They couldn't hear a word that was being said between Oblivia and the men. Time was slipping away. They had to find a way to get closer.

Julia crept toward the house. She could see a door to the cellar that had been left open. Julia wedged herself between two old planks that kept it partially barred. "*Whoo, whoo*," she called. The boys turned and saw her. Julia waved for them to follow, then disappeared inside.

She had entered an amazing room. It felt as if she were in a submarine's engine room, or inside the workings of a giant clock.

Rick entered, then Jason. They stood with mouths agape, staring in disbelief. Everywhere they looked they saw toothed wheels, levers, pipes of every shape and length, iron boxes, and silent machines intricately connected to one another. The only open space was a narrow path in the middle of this maze of machines.

"It's not a house," Jason murmured. "It's a machine."

Rick shook his head. "No, it's a house — this must be the mechanism that makes the house turn."

They carefully worked their way to a small opening that was occupied by an old desk. On the desk rested some levers that, presumably, activated the gears. On the wall behind the desk was a control panel that had stylized drawings on it: One seemed to represent the house; another, the sun and moon. The rest indicated, by means of arrows, the direction in which the entire construction revolved. From the control panel, several pipes reached a series of vats of hot and cold water that disappeared on the other side of the wall.

"You guys get the feeling that the last person who lived here was named Dr. Frankenstein?" Julia whispered.

Rick cleaned the dust off the levers on top of the desk. He tried to figure out how they were used. "These could be used to control the hot water," he surmised. "These, um, these could be used to control the energy that's produced by the windmills on top of the hill."

"Right," Jason said, "but none of it matters anymore. This house had been abandoned. And from the looks of that wrecking ball outside, it sure seems like it won't be here much longer."

Faint voices trailed into the room from the front yard. "We can marvel at modern science later on," Julia said. "I think we'd better get moving if we want to hear what's being said outside. There's got to be somewhere we can go to spy on them without being seen."

Her eyes scanned the room. She noticed a staircase and went to it, climbing up and up. At the top there was a door.

A door covered with shards of mirrors.

Opening the door, with Jason and Rick behind her, Julia was startled to hear the thumping of drums. No, not drums — the beating of wings, the whoosh and swish of feathers in flight. The room was dark, but Julia could hear the birds, feel their presence all around her, as they rustled in the dim light.

"*Whooo, whoo, whoo!*" echoed in the shadows.

The kids stood perfectly still, waiting for the birds to quiet down. Then they slowly, cautiously entered a barren room, empty of all furniture. It had a strange odor. The ivy had penetrated the cracked windows, and now grew inside the house itself, giving the scene a feeling of unreality.

Moving on, they discovered a large room shaped liked a crescent moon. The stagnant air and odor

of decay was even stronger in this one. The smell was nearly unbearable. Jason made a gagging noise.

"Shhh!" Julia hissed. She pointed toward his ear and mouthed the word, "Listen!"

The voices coming from outside were now clear as a bell.

Julia moved carefully, aware of the strange sensation that she was being watched. She looked around and thought she saw, at the top of the stairs, a pair of yellow eyes staring at her.

"*Whooo, whoo, whoo!*" the owl cried into the shadows.

Jason and Rick had gone to the window that overlooked the front yard. The windows were tall and narrow, protected by iron bars. The glass panes were either cracked or missing entirely. Between the two large windows was the main entrance. Its door was rotted and dangerously teetering toward the outside of the house.

Again Julia heard the swishing of wings from the floor above. This room, too, was almost completely stripped of furniture. The only thing left was the skeleton of a large cuckoo clock, its inner parts strewn on the floor. There was also a small round table with a top carved in the shape of an owl. Julia thought of the yellow eyes and the fluttering of wings. *Owls*, she thought, *everywhere*.

Jason and Rick peeked outside. Oblivia and the men from the Cyclops crew were scrutinizing a piece of paper that was laid out on top of the hood of the truck.

"It's the map!" Rick said.

Oblivia was giving her final instructions. "You must demolish this entire house! But you need to proceed cautiously, one wall after another."

The foreman took off his cap. He scratched his bald head behind the ear. "Look, lady, that could be a little tricky. You see . . ."

"No," Oblivia snapped. "You keep telling me why you can't do this, why you can't do that. Enough excuses. You must help me find that door!"

"That's what we don't get," one of the men said. "If it's just a door, why not walk around the house and find it?"

"Yeah," another chimed in, tapping his temple with a sausage-like finger. "Maybe it's in your imagination, lady."

With scarcely contained rage, Oblivia hissed, "The door is hidden — hidden long ago. This map leads me to believe that it was covered over, buried inside one of the walls, hidden in the cellar — I don't know. Finding it is your job!" She held fast to

Thomas Bowen's map, her long fingernails clutching it like the talons of a predatory falcon.

The foreman raised his hands, as if to say, "Whatever you say, lady." Next to him, Manfred smirked. He was clearly glad to see someone else be the target of Oblivia's wrath.

"Okay, we gotcha, lady. So once we find the door, what next?" the foreman asked.

Oblivia smiled. "Then your work is done," she said, "and my work begins."

The four men looked at one another, perplexed. This was the strangest job they'd ever had.

"Look, Ms. Newton," the foreman said, trying to take a conciliatory tone. "The house is yours, the money is yours, so I'm not trying to tell you what to do."

Oblivia nodded. "But?"

"But I need you to understand that it could be dangerous," he continued. "This isn't a normal house. The walls are made of aluminum and wood. The roof is made of mirrors! This place has so many pipes and gadgets, we're going to have to take it nice and slow, if you know what I mean."

Oblivia laughed mockingly. "Afraid, are you? This is a toy house, the product of a harmless clock-maker's daydreams. Pure foolishness! A house that turns! Absurd!"

Inside the room, Rick smiled. He had been right. The house did turn. And of course, aluminum made sense. The house had to be strong but still light enough to move.

"Well, I'll admit," the foreman said, scratching behind his ear again. "I've never seen anything like it in my life, and I've been around the block a few times. Who built this place, anyway?"

"A little man named Peter Dedalus," Oblivia replied.

Hearing that name, Rick's pulse quickened.

One of the workers dared to speak up one final time. "This job doesn't feel right," he complained. "This house is a jewel, a masterpiece of craftsmanship. It don't feel right to tear it apart."

"That's enough of that, Paul," the foreman said. "Ms. Newton can do with it what she likes. We're just hired help around here. Got it? Let's get to work. It's demolition time."

With those words, a desperate thrashing of wings banged and crashed through the room.

The men looked warily at the house.

"I think maybe there's some kind of creature in there," one of the workers said.

"Just . . . do . . . it," Oblivia ordered.

The men nodded, grumbling in agreement. They

picked up their tools. The foreman said, "We'll take one last look around inside, then we'll start."

The boys quickly retreated from the window. Startled, Julia lost her balance and inadvertently leaned on the owl table behind her. The table produced a metallic noise. And it moved, as if taking a step back on its legs.

Julia stood petrified. She stared at the table wide-eyed, unable to come up with a logical explanation. Did that really happen? Was it just her imagination?

"Um, Rick?"

"What?"

"This table . . . it kind of just moved by itself," Julia explained sheepishly.

"You probably knocked into it," Rick reasoned.

"No, it moved," Julia insisted.

Jason peered through the window again. The men were bustling about in the back of the truck, gathering tools and equipment for the job ahead. But where had Oblivia and Manfred gone, Jason wondered? He couldn't see them.

His heart skipped a beat when he spotted them again. Oblivia and Manfred had left the construction crew. They were headed toward the front door!

Away from the men, Oblivia stopped to confide in Manfred. "We'll find it soon," she purred with satisfaction. "Without the map, I could have searched for the door all my life without success. But now, here it is. Imagine, it was in Peter's house all the while! Wonderful! I've never felt better in my life!"

Julia was still immobile in the center of the room.

"Rick, I'm not kidding," she said. "I barely touched it, and this weird little table . . . it took a step backward!"

She looked up at him, eyes wide. "It's freaking alive!"

Just outside the main door, Oblivia again unrolled Thomas Bowen's map. She studied it, then rolled it up and tucked it under her arm.

"How long are those good-for-nothings going to take?" she muttered. "What is it, teatime already?"

Manfred frowned and began scrutinizing the front door. "Maybe I can get things started," he said, rolling up his sleeves.

On the opposite side of the door, Jason remained still. He caught Rick's eye and jerked his head as if to say, *come here, now!*

Oblivia planted her hands on her hips. She looked up at the mirrored roof.

"We'll start from the top," she decided. "From that ridiculous roof. Listen to that racket! What are those things? Owls and their filthy droppings? Ugh,

where are those men? Come on, you idiots!" she muttered.

Manfred gently tested the strength of the front door. It was locked, but badly rotted.

"Easy," he sniggered.

Just inches away, Rick and Jason held their breath, not knowing what to do.

Meanwhile, Julia looked at the top of the stairs. A large white-feathered owl had suddenly appeared. It stared at her, perched on the handrail as immobile as a statue.

Julia brushed against the round table. . . .

Suddenly Rick knew what to do. He pushed hard against the front door, driving it dangerously into Manfred, who raised his hands to keep from getting crushed.

Oblivia screamed.

Jason instantly understood. He, too, threw himself against the huge door, pushing it toward Manfred. With a loud moan, the hinges ripped out of the frame and the door slammed down on Manfred's head and shoulders, driving him to the ground.

Julia's owl lifted off, gliding through the room.

"Run!" yelled Jason, calling for his sister. "If they find us, we're dead!"

Julia was still frozen beside the table. She touched

it. It was cold and covered with dust. Not alive, of course not. The snowy owl spread its wings and glided out the opening where the front door had stood.

The boys reached her. Jason pulled on her arm. "Hurry," he urged.

"The owl," she tried to explain. "The table . . . and then . . . it appeared at the top of the stairs."

Jason cut her off abruptly. "Julia, listen to me. We've got to get out of here. Before they find us! Now!"

Julia seemed to snap out of her reverie. She blinked, focusing on Jason, then Rick. Nodded *yes, now, let's run.*

They fled the room, thundering down the stairs. But a moment before going down, Rick noticed that on the dusty floor, near the table, there were four perfectly round circles, lighter than the rest.

As if the table had moved by itself.

CLARK BEAMISH
STATION

Jason, Rick, and Julia ran down the stairs, bolted out the door, and plunged into the dense thicket. Rick found the hidden path and led them away from the house. Panting and out of breath, they didn't stop until they reached the broken gate. They fell into the tall grass, hidden from sight. Rick lifted his head, afraid that someone might have seen them.

In the distance, they heard the motor of the demolition crane starting up. And in that moment, lying in the grass, the three kids felt utterly helpless. There was nothing they could do.

Then something strange happened. A cloud of owls circled above the mirrored roof, around and around again.

"That's not normal," Julia whispered.

"How many do you think there are?" Jason wondered. "Dozens?"

The nocturnal birds, disturbed by the noise of the crane, swooped nervously around the house. They poured out of the second-story window. They glided over the front lawn, letting out mournful cries.

"It's like they're trying to defend the house," Rick said. "What are we doing here? We've got to help them!"

Rick moved to stand up. Julia grabbed his arm.

"No," she said, shaking her head sadly. "It's over. We lost."

"Let's get out of here!" Jason said. "I can't stand to see it. There's nothing we can do. It would be too dangerous for us to be found out now."

Rick hesitated, staring at the top of the crane that was beginning to move, slowly, steadily, toward the house.

"I hate her," he seethed.

The great iron ball crashed against the mirrored roof, shattering whatever peace remained.

The children stood paralyzed. Every time the ball hit the house, their stomachs tightened into knots. "We have to go now," Jason said. "We'll find another way to help."

Without speaking, Julia and Rick agreed. They found their bikes and rode away from the house, trying hard not to look back, or listen to the crunching, crushing sounds of a great home — a work of art, really — being destroyed by greed.

"I'd like to demolish *her*," Julia grumbled, throwing a rock into the bay. They had stopped alongside the road, heads still spinning, hearts still racing.

Rick rationed the last few drops of water. He

offered a sip to Jason, who shook his head, dejected. He had a blade of grass between his teeth and was gnawing at it angrily.

"We were right, you know," he finally said.

"What?" Rick said.

"About the map," Jason said. "We were right."

Rick nodded thoughtfully. "We were also right about the doors. Now there are three," he said, "*at least* three."

"We've got to get that map," Jason repeated for maybe the twentieth time that day. "We need to find all the doors. We have to figure out what's going on."

No one had the heart to say it, but the group had no intention of going to Oblivia Newton's house as they had originally planned. It was as if, by seeing the demolition of Mirror House, they had realized what they were up against. A ruthless enemy who would stop at nothing. She was dangerous. It would be a grave mistake to take her lightly.

"Why do you think she wants another door?" Julia asked. "I mean, isn't the one at Miss Biggles' house enough?"

"That's a good question," Jason said, holding his head in his hands. "Add it to the long list of things we don't know," he groaned. "I can't make head or tails out of anything anymore! What does Oblivia really want? What are these doors all about? Where are they? How do they work?! Who put them here in the first place?!"

Julia and Rick exchanged glances. It was almost funny, in a way. Jason could get so emotional sometimes.

Rick finally confessed. "I knew the owner of that house."

"What?!" Jason said.

"Oblivia said it belonged to the clockmaker of Kilmore Cove," Rick explained. "Peter Dedalus. He had a shop on Sweet Treat Lane. I remember going there with my dad. It was on my first day of grade school. We walked to his shop. I don't know why I didn't notice it at first, but now I remember where I saw the drawing on the Owl Clock sign before."

"What drawing?" Julia asked. "The owl?"

"A white owl," Rick said, "with a clock in his beak. It was the sign on top of his shop. It said PETER DEDALUS: WATCHES, CLOCKS, PENDULUMS, AND OTHER USELESS TIME STEALERS."

Rick looked up at Jason and Julia, who were listening attentively. "On top of the door, there was one of those little bells that ring every time someone comes in the door. Funny how you remember little

things. Anyway, all the stores have them these days, but back then, the clockmaker was the only one who did. I loved that chime; it just sounded like . . . magic. I remember opening and closing the door, over and over again, just to hear the bell ring." Rick smiled at the memory.

Julia smiled, too. "It's nice," she said. "I like your story, Rick. Please tell us more."

"Well, my father had to pull me away. He took me to the counter. It seemed so very, very tall. I must have been really small back then," Rick recalled. "The only things in the glass case were clocks: big clocks, small clocks, clocks of every imaginable shape and design. The watchmaker, Peter Dedalus, was in the back of the store. There was a drape separating it from the main room, and I remember that I could hear music. Beautiful music. I had never heard it before, or heard it since. But I know that if I heard it again, I'd recognize it."

"What was he like, the watchmaker?" Jason asked.

Rick shrugged. "A short man with a very long nose," he said with a laugh. "To be honest, I was too interested in the clocks to notice. I remember my dad introducing us, saying, 'Peter, I brought you my son.' He asked Peter Dedalus to make a watch for me."

Rick unhooked a wristwatch from his bike's handlebar and showed it to the twins. "The band needs to be replaced," Rick said, "but Dedalus is gone now."

Julia held the watch, fascinated. It was square and had the design of a white owl in the center. Under the owl, the initials of its maker were inscribed: P.D.

"It's beautiful," Julia said. "A nice watch, and a beautiful memory."

"It still keeps perfect time," Rick said. "He did very good work, Mr. Dedalus."

Jason stood, restless. "And now . . . right at this moment," he said, "his house is being destroyed."

"Oh great, just when I was feeling a little better," Julia said. "Remind me not to invite you to my next birthday party."

Her brother laughed. "I always go to your birthday parties!" He grabbed a fistful of grass and playfully threw it at her. "They're my birthday parties, too!"

"So what happened to him?" Julia asked Rick. "You said he's gone now."

"Nobody knows," Rick said. "That's the strange part. One day he just disappeared. At least, that's what my mom told me."

"He vanished?" Jason asked. "Poof, and that's it?"

"That's it," Rick answered. "He left the store and

never came back. He didn't move his stuff or anything."

It instantly dawned on Jason what might have happened. "Maybe he found the door!"

"What?"

"Maybe he can't get back!" Julia chimed in. "He could have discovered the door in his house, opened it, and never come back!"

"I don't know," Rick said doubtfully.

"Or maybe he got hurt," Jason said darkly. "You've seen what our friends back there are capable of."

Julia grabbed her bike. "Speaking of time, boys, it's time to move."

"Oh yeah, where to?" Rick asked.

"You are going to show us that store," she said. "I'd be curious to take a look around."

- Chapter 13 -
FIGHTING BACK

"Can't you be more careful, Manfred? This is no time for fooling around!" Oblivia hissed.

After extricating him from beneath the heavy front door, the Cyclops workers brought Manfred to a cool patch of grass at a safe distance from the house, suggesting that he sit quietly and rest. Manfred, however, refused to act like a model patient. He gritted his teeth. His stomach was churning, and his head reeled with hostile thoughts.

His clothes were soiled with dust and splinters. His nose had begun to bleed again, forcing him to apply pressure by holding a handkerchief against it. His new sunglasses had been shattered, the second pair in two days!

He turned to Oblivia and snorted something incomprehensible.

"Would you explain what got into your head?" Oblivia asked. "Getting a door to fall on your face! You could have gotten killed!"

"It didn't hurt that much," Manfred said, a little untruthfully. (It hurt like the dickens, but he'd never admit it.) "Besides, I'm not so sure it *was* an accident!"

Oblivia snickered. "Oh, the house attacked you, did it?"

"I heard footsteps," Manfred claimed.

"You saw stars, is more like it." Oblivia laughed. "Oh, don't look so disappointed, Manfred. You probably heard those birds. What an unholy racket!"

The demolition ball hit the top of the roof with a crash. The solar panels that formed the roof shattered. Walls tumbled, supporting beams snapped in half. Then the workers stopped the crane while two men quickly checked the house. They were searching for the door. After failing to find it, they signaled to the crane operator again — bring the wrecking ball one more time!

And so it went, slowly but surely, to Oblivia's great pleasure.

"I've got to admit," Manfred said, watching the destruction, "it looks like fun."

Just then, the wrecking ball hit a corner wall. For no apparent reason, it got stuck. The workers tried to dislodge it by hand.

Suddenly, with a loud mechanical whine, the entire structure of the house began to turn. Somehow, despite all the damage, it was working again. It was as if an emergency button had been accidentally pushed, activating the rotation of the house.

"What are they doing now?" Oblivia complained to Manfred. "The whole house is turning! It's ridiculous!"

Now the chain that connected the ball to the crane began to get taut. One worker waved frantically at the crane operator. "Shut it down!"

"This is getting interesting," Manfred observed, quite entertained. "If the house keeps turning . . . and if the chain doesn't break . . . it might pull over the whole crane, kaboodle and all. Quite a show, don't you think, Ms. Newton?"

Oblivia stood horrified, speechless, watching the disaster unfold.

"I'm glad I parked the motorcycle on the other side," Manfred said.

There was a horrific noise.

The crane, folding itself in two, was pulled to the ground by the turning House of Mirrors. It was as if the house was fighting for its life.

- Chapter 14 -
THE TELLING-TIME
DOOR

Legend has it that Sweet Treat Lane derived its name from the aptly-called Sweet Treat Pastry Shop, located at the corner of the narrow alley. The shop had two enormous glass windows: one facing a narrow alley and the other facing the main square of Kilmore Cove. The windows were covered with lace curtains that partly hid its precious treasures — cream puffs, pastries, butter cookies, chocolate confections, and creamy truffles. Once inside, the sweet fragrance of vanilla, cinnamon, cocoa, and powdered sugar filled the air, making customers weak-kneed with hunger.

Julia, Jason, and Rick momentarily forgot their troubles thanks to an enormous rack of raisin scones, strawberry cream puffs, and chocolate-covered doughnuts. They ate standing under the sign in front of Peter Dedalus' clock shop, passing the bag to one another until they had devoured every crumb.

The sign of the white owl with a watch in its beak was still there, but the shop windows were completely boarded up. The entrance was protected by a massive door reinforced by an iron gate. The center of the gate had a panel that contained an extremely intricate, and downright bizarre-looking, lock.

A sign had been attached to the gate with wire:

GOING OUT OF BUSINESS!
EVERYTHING MUST GO!
PHONE ***555-0020
(ENTER FROM REAR)

The children went around to the back. They crossed a stone archway, entered a dimly lit alley, and emerged on a small patio at the rear of the store. They found a modern door, quite unlike most doors in downtown Kilmore Cove. Strangely, the door had recently been cemented into the wall, as if to patch an opening. The cement was ugly and did not fit well with the rest of the building. It looked more like a barricade to prevent entering than a real door.

"Okaaay," Julia drawled, "that's weird."

"Nothing is ever easy," Rick groaned.

"Yep," Jason agreed, "and that's half the fun!"

They tramped back to the front of the store. Rick bent down to examine the lock.

"This has got to be Peter's handiwork," he mused.

"You mean, like, another one of his nutty inventions," Julia stated.

"I think I understand," Rick said. "Imagine that Peter . . . disappeared. I bet that nobody could figure out how to beat this lock, so they banged a hole

through the wall in the back. That's why that new door is cemented there — to cover the hole."

"It's a good theory," Jason said.

"Peter Dedalus was famous for inventing intricate mechanisms like this lock," Rick told the twins. "He loved to create little inventions that could perform impossible tasks. Mechanical arms that transcribed musical scores . . . robotic hands that took the eggs off the stove . . . beds that made themselves . . ."

"Like the owl table at his house!" Julia exclaimed.

"I've been thinking about that, Julia," Rick said. "You may be right. Maybe you weren't dreaming. I remember that my mother once told me about a sitting room that had robotic chairs that moved around the room."

The panel in the middle of the gate was absolutely original. There was no keyhole or, it appeared, anything else that might be used to unlock the gate. There was, instead, the face of a clock with two very long hands, a perpetual calendar on the upper part of a crescent moon, and two ring bolts, one on each side.

Jason tried to turn the one on the right. It still worked! The hands of the clock moved in response. The other bolt was apparently used to wind the clock.

"Everything he ever built worked to perfection," Rick noted. "This lock works, I'd bet my life on it, but we don't know its secret."

"I wouldn't say that," Julia observed. "Look at the year in the calendar. It's way off."

"Hmmm," Rick mused, frowning. He found it hard to believe that the great watchmaker would make such a mistake.

"What time is it?" Jason asked.

"Four-fifteen," Rick replied.

"Maybe we need to set the correct time and wind it up," Jason suggested. He changed the clock to 4:15 and gave the bolt a few turns.

Nothing happened. "Dumb idea, I guess," Jason said.

"No," Julia said. "You might be on to something. I mean, well, it kind of makes sense. Don't you think, Rick?"

"Nothing has made sense around here since I met you guys," Rick joked. "But, sure, the time on the clock just might have something to do with opening the lock. It would be the type of thing that a watchmaker might invent."

"Maybe you didn't wind it up enough," Julia suggested.

Jason frowned and held up a reddened thumb.

He sighed, then continued winding the brass ring. "Maybe we should have gone to Argo Manor. I bet Nestor knows something about Dedalus and his House of Mirrors. He always seems to know more than he lets on."

"Probably," Rick said, "but if he does, he's been keeping the secrets to himself. I think if we want to find out what's really going on with the doors, we've got to discover it for ourselves — the hard way."

"So who hid the doors, anyway?" Julia asked. "Ulysses Moore?"

"No," Jason answered. "He's the one who left us clues to find the doors. He's the one who's helping us!"

Julia was not convinced. She watched Jason wind the clock for a few minutes, then finally concluded, "Well, I guess that didn't do the trick, either."

Suddenly the hands of the clock began to move. The numbers on the perpetual calendar began to roll. The clock hands repositioned themselves on a different hour. The calendar showed a new year; it now pointed to the year 1206.

"At least it's doing *something*," Jason replied, encouraged. He had another idea, thinking that maybe the number of the year was a clue, telling them how to set the clock. The year 1206 could be read as a time of the day: six minutes after twelve o'clock. He changed the hands on the clock to 12:06 and wound it once more.

Again, the hands spun on the clock's face and the calendar rolled to a new number: 334.

"Aaaarrrgh!" Jason yelled in frustration. "I can't take it anymore. Secret codes, tarot cards, now this! It's one brain-buster after another!"

"Maybe we're overthinking things," Rick offered. "Let's try phoning the number on the sign. Maybe somebody will come and open up for us."

"It's worth a shot," Julia agreed. "Let's find a store where they'll let us borrow their phone."

"Not yet," Julia admitted to Ms. Calypso. "We want to read the books you sold us, but we've been really busy!"

The petite woman turned to Rick. "Too busy to read? But it rained all last night. What in the world could be keeping you three so busy that you can't read a few pages?"

"Just, um, stuff," Rick said.

"Do you really want to know the truth, Ms. Calypso?" Julia interrupted, giving a dramatic sigh.

Ms. Calypso smiled approvingly. "Yes, of course."

Rick stared at Julia, trying to guess her intentions. "The truth is," he said, fumbling to think of something, "I've been reading a different book. It's called *The Crocodile and the Long-Lost Map*."

"Oh?"

"Yeah," he said, nodding emphatically. "It's about Egypt . . . and Tutankhamen . . . and, see, he gets lost inside the House of Life."

"The what?" Ms. Calypso asked.

"It's like this labyrinth . . . a great museum, sort of, for like . . . everything!" Rick explained lamely.

"Hmmm," Ms. Calypso clucked, "I'd be curious to read this book."

"Oh, I'll loan it to you," Rick offered, piling one lie unsteadily on top of the other.

"Hey," Julia said, snapping her fingers. "I just thought of something. Could I please use your phone, Ms. Calypso?"

The pay phone was tucked behind the cash register. Julia lifted the receiver, slid in a coin, and dialed. Around the corner, Ms. Calypso was eagerly showing the boys a long list of books that they absolutely had to read.

The phone rang and rang. Julia glanced distractedly

along the shelves. There was a pile of books that had been special ordered. Books that needed to be picked up. On one shelf, the lowest, Julia spied a red velvet book. A note on top of it had only three large question marks scribbled on it, as if Ms. Calypso didn't know where to file it or who ordered it. Julia couldn't resist taking a look at it. The book was old, its pages yellowed with age. The cover page had a photograph of a porch.

What intrigued her most, however, was the title:

The Curious Traveler
A Mini-Guide to Kilmore Cove and Its
Surroundings

Julia quickly glanced up. Good, Ms. Calypso and the others were still talking. No one was watching her. She tried leafing through the book, but its pages were still uncut, as if no one had ever read it. How strange. When she opened the front cover, however, a solitary sheet of paper fell out. Reaching to catch it, Julia leaned forward too swiftly and dropped the receiver with a bang.

"Is everything all right?" called Ms. Calypso.

Julia grabbed the paper, glanced at it, and quickly slipped the paper into her back pocket. She replaced

the guide on the shelf. Standing up straight, she smiled innocently at Ms. Calypso. "Sorry," Julia whispered. "I'm a klutz."

Then Julia held up a finger, as if listening to a voice on the phone.

"Hello? Good afternoon," Julia said, pretending to have a conversation for the benefit of Ms. Calypso. "Yes, I'm calling about Peter Dedalus, the watchmaker's shop. Uh-huh, I understand. Sure, no problem." Julia smiled at Ms. Calypso, shrugging her shoulders. "No, don't worry about it. Thank you very much."

Julia hung up the receiver. She glanced down to see that the book was back in its original place, then rejoined the others on the other side of the counter.

"So?" Jason asked.

"So nothing," Julia replied. "The office was closed. The person who finally answered was the cleaning lady — and she didn't know anything."

"Really?" Ms. Calypso said suspiciously. "That seems unusual, even by Kilmore Cove standards."

"We really have to go!" Jason announced. "We promised Nestor that we wouldn't be late. Isn't that right, guys?"

"Right, right, oh yeah, got to run," Rick and Julia

replied. They quickly thanked Ms. Calypso and hurried out of the bookstore.

The woman stood at the window, looking after the three children. "Most unusual," she mused to herself. She wondered what they were really up to — and why on earth they'd be interested in a store that had been closed for years.

A few moments later, a nondescript woman entered the shop. She went straight to the romance section and selected a book with a red cover.

"This is the one," she said, sure of herself.

"Excellent choice," agreed Ms. Calypso. She tapped a few keys on the cash register.

The old machine started ticking, like a pendulum clock. At the end of the transaction, a little mechanical man took off his hat, and the receipt slid out from beneath his feet.

"What a perfectly charming register!" exclaimed the woman. "It must be an antique!"

"Yes, and it still works perfectly," Ms. Calypso replied. Her fingers gently touched the round copper keys. "It was built by a local artisan right here in town."

The customer left. That's when Ms. Calypso looked at the public phone. Strange, the change to make the call had been returned.

That's mysterious, she thought, puzzled. *The call that Julia made . . . didn't take any money? I wonder how that could be?*

As soon as the kids left Calypso's Island, Julia began to run. She stopped only when she got to the alley on Sweet Treat Lane.

"What's the big hurry?" Jason asked, panting heavily.

Julia took a piece of paper from her back pocket. She handed it to Jason. "I found this inside an old guide to Kilmore Cove."

It was a drawing. A pencil sketch of a train coming out of a tunnel. Under the sketch were these words:

What happens to the cars after the tunnel?

On the opposite side, there was a sketch of the statue of the King of England, the same statue they had passed earlier that morning. Below it, someone had scribbled:

No one named King William V ever ruled England!

"What does that mean?" Rick asked. "Is this a clue — or a joke?"

"I have no idea if William the Fifth really existed," Julia admitted. "I think I slept through that part of school."

"What part was that?" Rick asked. "September through June?"

"Hardy-har-har," replied Julia, rolling her eyes.

"Seriously," Rick said. "Why would there be a statue of a king who never existed?"

"And besides that," Jason added, "a statue that looks an awful lot like a young Nestor?"

"Now you're talking crazy-talk," Julia said.

"Hey," Jason replied, hands held out, "this whole town is crazy, if you haven't noticed."

"What do you make of this, about the tunnel?" Julia asked. "Is that like a riddle?"

Rick shook his head. "I haven't got a clue."

Jason walked to the front of Peter Dedalus' gate. "There's got to be a way to get inside this store!" he grumbled.

"So there was no answer at that number, then?" Rick asked Julia.

"Nope," Julia answered. "It just rang and rang."

"We need the help of a ghost — a ghost named Ulysses Moore," Jason declared.

"Oh no," Julia groaned to Rick. "Here we go. He's leaving planet Earth again."

"I'm serious," Jason insisted. "I still believe that

Ulysses Moore hasn't abandoned us. Somehow, some way, he's trying to help us discover the truth. We couldn't have made it this far without some kind of help."

Julia sighed. There was no arguing with Jason, not when he got like this. The only thing to do was to play along. "Okay, fine, figure it out then! It's your move, genius."

Jason scowled. "We agree the key to opening the door is with this clock."

Rick nodded. "So what have we learned?" he asked rhetorically. "The year 334 was wrong. But the month and day on the calendar are right. Maybe that means . . . that . . . the year isn't really a year?"

"Huh?" Julia said.

"We've been acting like it's a year," Rick said, newly enthusiastic. "But maybe those numbers stand for something else. Maybe that number is a clue."

Julia slumped down on the curb. "I feel a headache coming on," she muttered.

Jason and Rick ignored her. "Maybe we need to reset the clock in a way that corresponds to the number of the calendar," Rick theorized. "If we look at this clock like it's a standard combination lock, then maybe the perpetual calendar provides the correct number sequence. What do you think, Jason?"

"Let's try it!" Jason agreed.

The boys attempted various sequences, first setting the clock to 3:34, then adding, subtracting, and finally randomly attempting arbitrary times.

Nothing worked.

"What time is it?" Julia asked, stifling a yawn.

"Five o'clock on the nose," Rick answered.

"So try that," she suggested.

"First, let's change it to seventeen-hundred hours, military time," Rick said. "Then we'll add three hundred and thirty-four to that . . . and we get . . . um . . ."

"Two thousand and thirty-four," Julia said in a bored tone.

Rick looked down at her in surprise.

Julia shrugged. "I guess I was awake for math."

Jason set the clock for 20:34, military time, which meant 8:34 P.M. Rick wound up the clock.

BZZZZZT!

The panel buzzed, but did not open. Again the hands revolved; the calendar now pointed to the number 116.

"Nothing," Jason cried in exasperation. "Where's a sledgehammer when you need one?" he groaned.

Rick kept at it, refusing to surrender. A minute had passed, he figured, so he added 1701 to 116.

"That's one thousand eight hundred and seventeen," Julia calculated absently.

"Or six o'clock, seventeen minutes," Rick said.

"Okay, eighteen seventeen is six seventeen P.M.,"
calculated Rick.

He quickly turned the ring, winding the clock in
haste.

BZZZZZT!

"Ugh, not again," Jason muttered.

But he was wrong.

The door clicked open!

- Chapter 15 -
THE LIGHTHOUSE KEEPER

As he bent over in the gardens of Argo Manor, Nestor heard the sound of footsteps on gravel. A shadow loomed over him.

He slowly turned to find himself face to face with Leonard Minaxo.

"Hello, Nestor," said the lighthouse keeper in a deep voice. His trousers were soaked to the knee. He wore a leather patch over his right eye. His face was rough — a tapestry of ruts, scars, and wrinkles. Minaxo's enormous hands were gnarled, as if chewed up by a lifetime of working at sea — lifting nets, pulling oars, facing whatever nature threw at him.

"Leonard," Nestor said, getting to his feet. "Where did you come from?"

Minaxo pointed to the cliff. "I came up the stairs," he answered, "seeing that you haven't gotten around to installing an elevator."

Nestor walked to the steep staircase and peered over the edge. He saw the fishermen's boat on Argo Manor beach.

"So?" Nestor asked expectantly. "Any news?"

"Nothing," Minaxo replied. His one eye was gray and restless. It wandered over the grounds, passed over the house, then returned to meet Nestor's gaze.

"Too much time has passed," the lighthouse keeper

stated. He glanced back at the house. "Are they inside?"

"No, they went to town," Nestor answered. "Or so they said."

"It's dangerous," Minaxo noted.

Nestor looked away. "There's no choice. . . ."

"You had a choice!" Minaxo said, his voice firm.

"There is something about them," Nestor began. "A rare quality. I want to believe."

Minaxo started whistling. A soft melodious tune, lilting, gentle, like a lullaby.

"No, Leonard," Nestor said, alarmed. "Stop it."

"Stop it," repeated the lighthouse keeper. "Yes, Nestor. How about that: Stop it."

Nestor set his jaw. He stood tall, chest out. "And did you climb all the way up here to tell me that?"

"I came to see the house again," Minaxo stated. "It has been a long time. And I came to tell you that we didn't find a key at the bottom of the cliff."

"We had to try," Nestor said softly, "even if the odds were not in our favor."

"Nor was there a body," Minaxo said.

Nestor looked up at Minaxo's face and nodded silently.

Earlier that morning, he had searched among the rocks and crevices. He went into the shallows,

looking for a trace of Manfred. Finding no sign of the man, Nestor concluded that he must have fallen into the sea. But wouldn't the tide have brought his body ashore, spit it out onto the beach?

Perhaps he survived after all, Nestor thought.

"Thank you, Leonard," Nestor finally said. "Thank you for trying."

Minaxo folded his arms across his massive chest. "We tried long before this day, my friend," he reminded Nestor. "And long ago we decided that it must end."

A crow flew overhead and came to rest on one of the branches of a sycamore tree. It seemed to study the men, a solitary black bird, a carrion, an eater of death.

Nestor gazed at the bird. *Death comes to us all*, he mused. *It is not important.* What is important, he decided, is how we live.

"Leonard . . ." Nestor began.

The lighthouse keeper grinned without pleasure. He held up a hand to silence Nestor. Then he lifted his face to the sun, closed his eyes, and recited a verse from memory:

One solitary king remained,
A king who must lose the game.
He seeks to win with three pawns,

Yet they will lose their lives . . .
and so the town mourns.

Nestor turned pale. "Is this one of your prophetic poems, Leonard?"

Minaxo shrugged. "You know that I am right."

"Is that a warning?" Nestor asked.

Minaxo tucked a thumb under his eye patch and flicked it up, revealing a hideous, sunken socket where an eye should be. He grinned mischievously. "You've got to see it my way, Nestor. Look at it from my perspective. Then you'll understand that the time to quit has long since passed. It's over, Nestor. Give up."

Nestor shook his head. He raised his voice, "I was given a job . . ."

"No!" Minaxo exploded. "You don't have a job, Nestor. No, you *had* a job. And you failed. And now we can't trust three children to do it for you!" Minaxo waved his arm violently, gesturing to the town and beyond. "The world has moved on without us," he fumed. "We're in the space age of satellites, computers, video games, and Palm Pilots! We're all connected now, haven't you heard? The World Wide Web, they call it. We're tangled up like flies for the feast, tied and bound in the spider's web."

"Always the poet," Nestor murmured, "isn't that right, Leonard? You always had a way with words."

Minaxo flipped down his eye patch.

"And a flair for the dramatic, I might add," Nestor noted. "But the fact remains: We cannot allow that woman to prevail."

"You poor, misguided soul," Minaxo said with a laugh. "Your quarrel is not with Oblivia Newton. She means nothing — nothing in the great scheme of things. Your quarrel, Nestor, is with the whole world! Progress, change, time itself! You should climb under a rock, you'd be happier! But the world keeps spinning, anyway, my friend. It goes on without you. Or have you forgotten what happened the last time? Don't you remember what was lost?"

Nestor swallowed. And he remembered. Every day of his life, every waking moment, he remembered all of it.

There was a long silence. The crow stretched its wings and lifted off the sycamore tree.

Leonard Minaxo laid a hand on the caretaker's shoulder. "I do not wish to be cruel, my friend. I'm sorry. I know that you suffer. But you needed to hear this before it was too late."

Nestor raised his eyes slowly until they met those of his friend. "But if I can't succeed," he said, almost pleading, "who will do it for us?"

"Certainly not three children," Minaxo spat.

"Why not?" Nestor said.

"Because . . . they just can't, that's why," Minaxo said, contemptuous of the mere thought. "They will surely fail."

Nestor tilted his head. "Are you so sure?" he asked. "Or have you grown afraid?"

"Ha!" Minaxo boomed in a great thunderous laugh. "I fear nothing. But I have foreseen the future. . . ."

"A poem," Nestor said. "Just a poem. The future is not frozen. Destiny still remains to be written." Nestor smiled. He shook Leonard's hand, thanked him, and said good-bye.

Nestor watched and waited until Minaxo climbed down to the beach and boarded the small fishing boat. He raised his arm, waved to his fishermen, then stood as silent and still as a statue for a long time.

He felt completely, utterly alone.

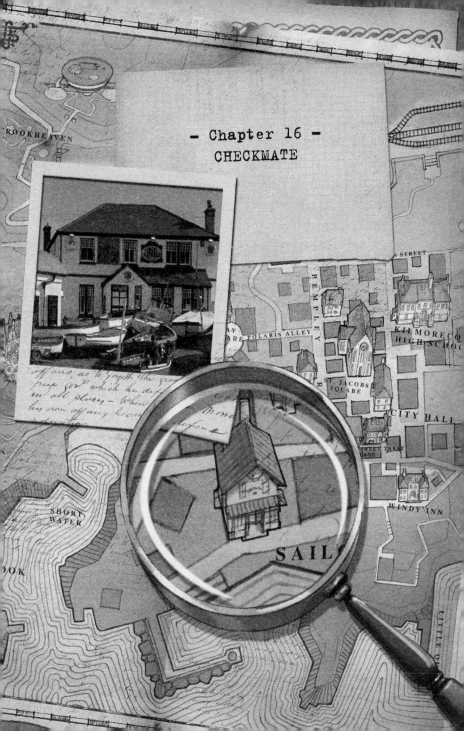

Rick paused, his hand on the door of Peter Dedalus' shop. He glanced around. No one was watching. Then he swiftly led Jason and Julia inside.

Inside the shop, everything was shrouded in darkness. But even in the faint light from the open door, they instantly saw that the room was in chaos.

Rick cautiously stepped forward. He found a small lamp and flicked the switch — and it worked.

"Let there be light," Jason intoned gratefully.

Large glass display cases stocked with watches and clocks formed a horseshoe around the perimeter of the room. It was as if the room had been turned upside down. Every drawer in every desk was either open or had been pulled out and thrown on the floor. Someone had obviously been searching for something. Paper was strewn on the floor, and the cash register was lying sideways against the showcase.

A dark curtain separated the main showroom from the workshop in the back, just as Rick remembered. He pulled it to the side. The back of the store was not in any better shape.

Rick fumbled in the dark, feeling around in a small closet. "Found you," he said. He triumphantly held a flashlight in his hand. "Figured there was one around here someplace," he explained.

"This place looks like it was hit by a monsoon," Julia said.

"Oblivia Newton," Jason muttered, remembering the House of Mirrors. "This is her handiwork."

Even so, the damage was not complete. Most items seemed unbroken. Watches, clocks, and small inventions remained. "No one ever cleaned the place out," Rick said with surprise. "They left all these treasures just lying here."

"Maybe she took what she came for," Julia guessed, "and left the rest."

"That's very possible," Rick whispered. "Whoever ransacked this place wasn't interested in most of this stuff. It's like they were looking for one thing . . . one very specific thing . . . and ignored the rest."

The watchmaker's tools lay in disarray, as if swept aside by an angry hand. A vinyl record collection had been dumped out and smashed on the floor. Yet a central display case, on the other hand, appeared to have weathered the storm practically untouched. It contained watches, a chessboard, a large desk clock, and other odd trinkets.

"They searched the drawers, scattered the papers, broke the records, but they didn't touch the watches or any of the priceless objects," murmured Julia. "If this was a robbery, that's the exact opposite of what you'd expect."

"Maybe you're right — they found what they wanted and decided to leave the rest," speculated Jason.

Rick walked back and forth in silence, contemplating the mess. "Why?" he wondered, filled with anger and bewilderment. "They destroy his store, tear apart his house . . . why? What do they want?"

Jason did not answer immediately, allowing Rick to vent his frustration. Then he quietly volunteered, "She wants power. She wants control of Kilmore Cove. She wants to possess all of the Doors to Time!"

Rick nodded, looking around the room with despair. His eyes fell on the display case. "Jason," he said in a whisper. "Do you still have that chess piece?"

"Sure," Jason answered, producing the metallic piece from his pocket.

Rick pointed to the chessboard in the case. "It belongs to that set," he said in a hush.

Rick opened the case and pulled out a large chessboard. It was about four inches thick and made of two different types of wood, alternating light and dark squares. And there were a few chess pieces that matched the one Julia had found behind the painting in Dr. Bowen's kitchen.

"That's some coincidence," Julia remarked.

"I don't believe in coincidences. Not anymore," Rick replied.

"They knew each other," Jason surmised. "Peter Dedalus and Penelope Moore were friends."

"Another puzzle to solve," Rick murmured, staring at the few pieces that remained on the board.

The chess piece in their possession was a white queen. Judging from the positioning on the board, it appeared that black had the tactical advantage over white.

"We shouldn't touch anything," Rick said. "It looks like an active game."

Julia studied the position of the chess pieces. "It would help if we knew whose move was next," she said.

"Who do you think was playing?" Jason asked. "Peter and Penelope?"

"Could be," Julia said. "And if Penelope had the white queen, it stands to reason that Peter was black."

Jason looked at the chessboard. It was one game in which he never had much interest. It was too slow and tedious.

Julia, however, did not find chess boring. She played for many hours with her father; it was one of the few passions that they shared. She said, as much to herself as to the others, "Isn't it cool to think that time stopped here? We're looking at a game that

started years ago. And it stopped ... never to be finished ... always in the middle, trapped somewhere between the beginning and the end."

"I think it was white's turn," said Rick suddenly.

Julia looked at him in surprise. "Why would you say that?"

"Just a feeling I have," Rick answered. "I mean, think about Peter Dedalus. He was a precise little man. His life's work was all about perfection, getting little details just right."

"So?" said Jason.

"So," Rick replied, pointing to the chessboard, "I don't think he would have disappeared from Kilmore Cove without making his last move."

"That's a wild guess," Julia observed.

"It's the best I can offer," Rick said.

"Well, I've got an idea," Jason said. "What if I just pick up this white knight and ..."

The chessboard began to vibrate.

"Jason!" Julia said in alarm. "Put that piece back right now!"

Rick reached out and grasped Jason's arm. "No, wait!" he exclaimed. "It's too late now. Some kind of internal gizmo has been activated. Finish your move, Jason."

Jason gulped. "I don't know anything about chess," he whispered.

The chessboard began ticking like a clock, faster and louder.

"Jason, I think you reactivated the game," Rick said. "The chessboard needs you to complete the move. This ticking must be some sort of timer. Quickly, make your move."

"But I . . . don't . . ." Jason stammered.

"There!" Julia pointed to a square. "It will put the king into checkmate."

Jason put the knight in place. The chessboard immediately stopped ticking. And a small drawer flew open on the side of the board.

"You did it!" Rick cried. "You won the game!"

Julia peered into the open drawer.

There was something inside.

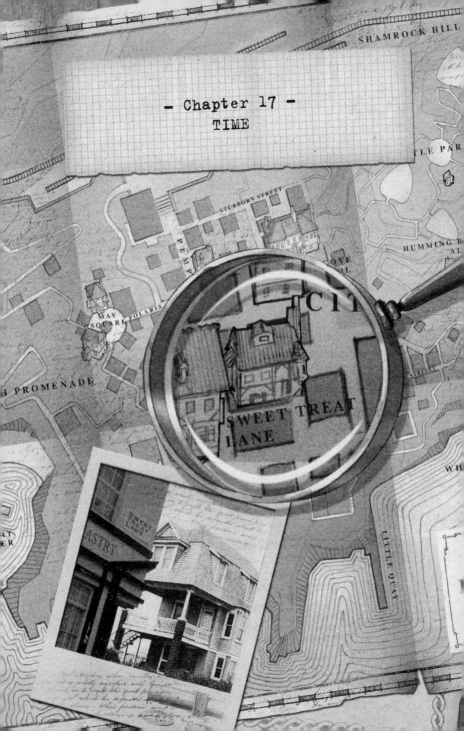

- Chapter 17 -
TIME

Nestor nervously checked his watch. He wandered aimlessly inside Argo Manor. *Where have those kids gone?* he wondered. It was almost six o'clock and they weren't back yet.

"It's dangerous," Leonard had said.

It was true that Leonard had an unnatural talent for foreseeing the future. Even with only one eye he could see better than most people. His poems hid meanings and messages that were often prophetic. Thinking about it, Nestor felt his stomach churn.

He was not a worrier by nature. But Jason, Rick, and Julia had been gone all day. Leonard's last verse kept swirling around in his head, spinning like a broken record:

> *He seeks to win with three pawns,*
> *Yet they will lose their lives . . .*

He thought of the broken-down bicycles the children had taken. "Where are you? Where have you gone?" muttered the old caretaker of Argo Manor.

He hobbled to his cottage to get a pair of powerful binoculars. He went to the cliff, scouring the coast of the town, searching for movement.

In the far distance, he saw Leonard disappear inside the white tower of the lighthouse. He thought back to Julia and Jason's mother, who had already called twice that afternoon. Both times the caretaker had to do triple somersaults to convince her everything was fine, everything was okay. "Safe and sound," he had said, "safe and sound."

But was it true?

"If they are harmed in any way," Nestor said out loud, "I will make you pay. Once and for all!"

At last, Nestor lowered the binoculars. Everything in Kilmore Cove seemed to be as usual. It was another typical Sunday in a sleepy town.

"Everything is fine," Nestor reassured himself. "They will return soon, safe and sound."

He just had to give it time.

Time . . .

Wasn't everything, in the end, a question of time?

A hundred feet below, the sea rumbled, crashing amongst the rocks. The branches of the sycamore, ash, and oak trees swung languidly in the wind. The seagulls rested on Argo Manor's roof before again taking wing.

Nothing stayed still.

Everything was fluid. Everything moved and changed, and time drove the wheel, time lit the fuse.

The keys had returned. The doors were opening again.

Who had put them back in circulation?

Did time itself turn the key? And was that his enemy after all? Was Leonard right? Should he just crawl under a rock? Surrender?

"Not even the keys stay still," Nestor murmured, sharing his thoughts with the sea of Kilmore Cove. "They move by themselves, forever seeking new locks to open. They go from hand to hand, pocket to pocket, drawer to drawer . . . until everyone has forgotten about them. When all seems quiet, they find themselves in new hands. And it begins anew. Always changing, always the same."

It was at that moment, while he was deep in thought, that Nestor heard a voice.

He turned to see Rick on his bike appear through the gate, followed by Julia and Jason.

"Nestor!" Julia exclaimed. "We found something. We found something!"

The old caretaker's heart leaped. A huge smile appeared on his face. Then he forced himself to be composed. He sighed, grumbled, and limped toward them.

"Back so soon?" he called out.

The kids were not to be denied. Too full of energy, enthusiasm, and excitement, they relentlessly peppered Nestor with question after question.

"Is it true there was never a King William V?"

"Did you know there's not one sign in Kilmore Cove with the name of the town?"

"Did you know that there are other Doors to Time?"

"Do you know a Cleopatra Biggles?"

"Have you heard of Owl Clock?"

"What do you know about Peter Dedalus?"

Nestor playfully covered his ears. "Stop with the questions," he demanded. "One at a time, one at a time."

Looking at Jason, Nestor knew that he had some explaining to do. He didn't have to answer every question, but he was going to have to respond to some of them.

"Peter Dedalus?" Nestor said. "Ah yes. He was a watchmaker — an inventor, I believe."

"Did he come to Argo Manor often?" Jason asked.

Nestor raised an eyebrow. "I don't recollect. Why do you ask?"

"He was friends with Penelope, wasn't he?" Julia asked, nodding her head.

Nestor coughed a few times, hoping for some sympathy. No such luck. The kids just watched him, waiting for answers. "Friend," he murmured, "is a big word. But, yes, I suppose you could say that they were acquaintances."

"You suppose?!" Jason said triumphantly. "Look what we found in his store!"

Jason thrust an envelope into Nestor's hands. In careful, perfect penmanship was written:

To my only friends
Penelope and Ulysses . . .
Even if too late.

Nestor was stunned. He turned the envelope over in his hands, not quite sure what to do with it. "You've already seen what's inside?" he asked the children.

"Read it for yourself," Rick urged.

"Don't you ever go home?" grumbled Nestor.

Rick laughed. "Yeah, occasionally."

"Before Rick goes," Jason said to Nestor, "we need to figure out how to listen to it!"

Nestor opened the envelope and pulled out a small, black, unmarked vinyl record.

"Where did you get this?" he demanded.

"We found it in his shop!" Julia answered.

"His shop?" Nestor echoed. "That's been closed for years. It's boarded up, cemented over, locked!"

Julia smiled at Rick and Jason. "Hey, where there's a will, there's a way."

A shiver of pride rushed down Nestor's back. He had been right about them. Each, on their own, was just a child, full of flaws and weaknesses. Yet together, they had a special quality. A rare determination and strength.

Jason, Rick, and Julia followed Nestor into Argo Manor. There was no escaping their desire to know more.

"I believe this record may answer the biggest secret of all!" Jason told Nestor enthusiastically.

"And what might that be?" Nestor asked. He climbed the staircase slowly, with the kids trailing behind.

"The mystery of Ulysses Moore, obviously!" Jason answered.

Nestor wheezed, coughing violently. "For that secret, you must only visit the cemetery," he snapped, holding a handkerchief to his mouth.

He led them into the library.

"Why is he bringing us here?" Julia whispered to Rick.

Nestor opened a large trunk that rested behind the leather sofa. He carefully took out the pieces of an ancient gramophone. "Let's see if this still works."

He handed Jason a brass horn, then lifted out the square box. Julia, in the meantime, was showing

Rick the family tree that was painted on the library's ceiling.

Nestor placed the base of the gramophone in the middle of the room. He enlisted Jason's help in assembling the amplifier. Finally, he put the vinyl record on the turntable, placed the needle on the record, and cranked the handle to start the old machine.

Initially, the only sound they heard was the light scratching and rhythmic tock-tock of the needle on vinyl. Until suddenly, a voice emerged.

The voice of Peter Dedalus.

The kids gathered around the gramophone, silent and expectant. Nestor leaned against the piano. Then, thinking better of it, he slumped onto the bench. For whatever he was about to hear next, Nestor decided, it was probably best if he was seated.

The record crackled to life:

Dearest Penelope, my good friend Ulysses, this is a cowardly way to get out of the game, but it's the only way I know how. I no longer have the strength or the courage to go on. Outside, the wind is blowing. A hard rain is falling. I think it's only fitting that my last day in Kilmore Cove should be a gloomy one. I ruined a great thing, and it's only now that I have fully realized what I have done.

The door beckons for me, offering a final escape. But before leaving, I must say this: I am honored to have been your friend. We and the others have shared a grand project. We were right to hide the keys, right to try to protect the doors. It was a noble attempt to try to save Kilmore Cove — and most importantly, the secret of the one who built it.

I will now make a confession. My weakness and my error bear the name and the face of a woman: Oblivia Newton. It's my fault that the project failed. No one else is to blame.

I will start from the beginning, so that you know the complete story. You deserve that much. I met her for the first time in my store on a Saturday afternoon. I saw her coming in through the curtain of my shop and figured that she was a tourist who had lost her way. The road still exists, even though we have eliminated every sign . . . and erased Kilmore Cove from every map . . . and even removed the train tracks. We worked so hard to erase every reference, every trace, every book that spoke of Kilmore Cove! The only thing left was Thomas Bowen's map, on which we had marked the position of the doors and their keys.

Our project was proceeding well. We had gathered almost all the keys. We had hidden the doors. Perhaps we could have erased every trace of the secret, if only Oblivia Newton had not entered my store. If only . . . I had not been so lonely, and so weak.

She was beautiful. A temptress! She had brought in something to appraise. It had been given to her by an old schoolteacher, Nessa Biggles, Cleopatra's sister.

Naturally, I knew Nessa well. But I was aghast to learn that she, who had been gone for so many years, would have given Oblivia one of our precious keys — the cat!

I could barely conceal my amazement. And I made a strategic error: I attempted to buy the key from her, perhaps with too much zeal. You remember, of course, how long we had searched. And suddenly, there it was, in my very store! Returned to Kilmore Cove in the hands of a marvelous stranger.

Oblivia sensed my desire for the key. She asked herself why a simple inventor would be so keenly interested in a simple key. She would not sell it. And then, over time, she began coming to my store with more frequency. She talked to me, we laughed, became friendly. This beautiful woman — coming to see me! Can you understand how that felt? One day, she followed me to Owl Clock. Eventually, she came into my house.

I was thrilled. I lived among my inventions, my tools, my ideas. The presence of a woman — a woman like that — inside my house was overwhelming. I showed her the House of Mirrors; she seemed fascinated by my every word, enthralled by everything I said. I made the house revolve for her, turning the window toward the sunset.

Oblivia told me countless times that I was a great genius, a marvel. And I, who had never truly known a woman before, believed her.

I was a fool, a pathetic dupe. I was blind to her true intentions. Oblivia knew that, sooner or later, I would reveal the meaning of the key. So she sought to earn my trust, lower my defenses . . . and she waited, like a spider spinning its web.

And I fell, oh how I fell, willingly, happily — without ever telling you. I will never forgive myself.

One night I blindfolded Oblivia and brought her into town. We used her key to open Miss Biggles' door. I guided her to the other side of the threshold! We stayed in Egypt less than an hour, but it was enough for her to understand.

Soon after we returned to Kilmore Cove, she asked if her key was the only one. I did not answer her, but she guessed the truth. There were other keys, and perhaps even other doors. A little at a time, in my innocence, my stupefied idiocy, I told her that Kilmore Cove had several doors, and that each had its own special key. I explained that each door was different from the other, and that each door opened to a different place, except for one, the central door, the one that was opened with four keys and would take you anywhere. I never told her of Argo Manor, but somehow she knew. And gradually her interest in me began to fade. She hungered, instead, for Argo Manor.

Oblivia became cold, distant. Her true nature was revealed. But by that time, it was too late. I could not turn back the hands of time. Ironic, is it not, for a watchmaker? Unable to manage time, though I spent my life at its mercy.

What was I to do? I'd betrayed everyone, including myself. Only one secret was left for me to protect, the biggest, one that not even you know.

The record turned for a while, silently. Nestor's eyes were closed. He caressed his beard, deep in thought. Then Peter's voice began again, but now it was more emotional, more confused, more racked with guilt.

I told her that . . . one of the ways to . . . open and close the doors . . . all of the doors . . . and to have complete control . . . only one key . . . and she . . . my Oblivia . . . asked if I knew where to find it . . . but I did not answer her . . . or break the promise.

So I flee! I will flee tonight, before she returns, while my mind is clear. I will go to where she will never find me. Ulysses, Penelope, I promise you that I kept the secret. She will never have control of all the doors!

Oh, my friends, I give you my love, and now I run — run from this world filled with lies and deceit. I once believed that the heart was the perfect machine, flawless in every way, but I discovered a more painful truth. Good-bye, brave Ulysses. Good-bye, sweet Penelope. You will receive by mail the lion's key. I no longer have need for it, for I shall never return. I gave my shop, and my house, to Oblivia. She wanted them and, well, I never could deny her anything. But I don't care. She can have them. That part of my life is over.

Erase my name. Blot me from your memory. Block me from your thoughts. But please know that I will never forget you!

With these words, the confession ended.

- Chapter 19 -
THE CHOICE

The sun had begun to set on the horizon; the sky had a tinge of orange-red as if something beyond the horizon was on fire.

In Argo Manor's library, the vinyl record crackled. Rick lifted the needle and replaced the arm.

Jason and Julia sat on the floor. Nestor stood, a faraway look in his eyes.

"So that's what happened," Julia said. "It was Peter who told Oblivia about the door!"

"It sounds like there are many doors," Jason corrected her. He was staring directly at Nestor.

Nestor coughed uncontrollably. Bent over, handkerchief held to his mouth — just a sick old man. He stayed like this, hunched in pain, until his cough subsided.

"Now we know why Oblivia is destroying the House of Mirrors," Rick announced. "She is looking for the door."

Alarmed, Nestor turned to Rick. "What is she doing?"

Rick told Nestor about what they witnessed on Owl Clock Road, the sad end to the amazing House of Mirrors.

"There wasn't anything we could do," Julia said, an apology in her voice. "We had to leave. It was too painful to watch."

"We are nearing the end," the old man said. He

walked toward the library door, looking for all the world like a dead man walking, depressed and defeated.

"Nestor, wait!" Julia called.

The old man stopped at the doorway. He did not look back, yet he did not leave.

"The key that Manfred took from your desk," Julia said, "what door did it open?"

"It was the lion," Nestor confessed. "The key that Peter spoke of. Ulysses gave it to me for safe-keeping."

"What door did it open?" Julia repeated, insistent.

"Peter's door," Nestor said with resignation. "The door in the House of Mirrors."

"Why did you hide the truth from us?" Jason demanded. "You should have told us!"

Nestor did not answer.

"Where does Peter's door lead?" Julia asked.

"How would I know?!" Nestor snapped.

"You had the key," Julia stated.

"You've always known more than you let on," Jason charged.

"I wish I had all the answers," Nestor said bitterly. "You make it sound easy. But you are wrong. The truth is a burden, a dull weight to carry. If I have spared you some of that, please forgive me."

There was a pause while the three children

absorbed what Nestor had just admitted. Julia, especially, felt sorry for the old caretaker. He was a quiet man who, if left alone, would simply like to plant flowers, pull weeds, and tend to beautiful gardens.

Rick spoke up, his voice full of logic and reason. "Okay, what do we know?" he asked. "Peter Dedalus said there were other doors in Kilmore Cove. One is here, in Argo Manor. Another is at Miss Biggles' house. A third is in the House of Mirrors." He paused, holding up three fingers on his right hand. "How many more doors are there, Nestor?"

The old man shrugged and shook his head.

"That's why we need the map," Jason said. "It shows all the doors and the keys that unlock them."

"Perhaps there is still . . . hope," Nestor said, looking up. He continued, "If she has the map, then Oblivia knows which keys she needs. But she does not have them all. Not yet. Ulysses Moore put them in a safe place. All of them, except Oblivia's original key — the one she got from Cleopatra's sister."

"And the one that Manfred stole from you last night," Jason said accusingly.

"Okay," Rick interrupted, "but that's all ancient history. It's over. There's no point placing blame. We need to focus on the present. Right now, Oblivia has two keys." He looked to Nestor. "Is that correct?"

Nestor nodded. "Yes, as far as I know," he added.

"We have four keys," Rick stated. "We still have the advantage."

Jason paced up and down. "We have to steal back her keys."

As they talked, Nestor stood in silence, observing these three young people. They had vigor, enthusiasm, confidence, purity. He remembered Leonard's poem — his prediction of failure and death — but he pushed it from his mind. Leonard had never met these kids. He could not look into their hearts. He could not see the truth and righteousness blazing in their eyes. Leonard did not know. He could not know.

Jason jarred Nestor's thoughts with a question. "Nestor, how many people know about the doors?"

"Besides me? Just Oblivia and Manfred," Nestor replied. "The others who once knew," he said, thinking of the past, "are all gone."

"You forget us," Rick said, looking to Jason and Julia. "We know, too. And we're on your side."

Nestor looked at the twelve-year-old boy who spoke with such conviction. Maybe he was not alone after all. Nestor wavered unsteadily at the doorway. He had to make a decision, but he feared that the wrong choice could lead to death.

He did not know what to do.

They were running out of time. To do nothing, he realized, would be cowardice. Evil cannot be ignored or wished away; it must be confronted and defeated. He had to do something.

Meanwhile, Rick — the organizer, the tactician — was attempting to come up with a plan. "The Moores had a mission. They tried to hide the doors and make sure the keys were safe. But they were betrayed by Peter Dedalus, who in a moment of weakness revealed the secret to Oblivia."

"That's where it gets really interesting," Jason said. "Peter ran away because he did not want to tell Oblivia the most important part of the secret. Isn't that right?"

"Yes," Julia said. "I remember his exact words: *Only one secret was left for me to protect.*"

Jason nodded. "It was hard to understand what he said after that, but it sounded to me as if there was one key, one key to control all of the doors. He knew where it was hidden, but Peter said that he would not break the promise!"

"So he fled," Nestor said, his voice strong and clear.

"Meanwhile, Mr. and Mrs. Moore died," Julia said.

"Maybe," Jason added.

"Whatever," Julia replied, rolling her eyes. "They sure don't seem to be around anymore. That's where we came in," she continued. "Our parents bought Argo Manor."

"And Oblivia flipped out," Rick said, smiling. "She was all set to take over, and you guys came along to spoil her plans!"

"We found the four keys," Jason said, his mood soaring now, happy. "Because we picked up the package at the post office! But do you remember why we got that package?" Jason asked Julia. "Because *somebody* left us that receipt tucked into the journal."

Nestor coughed. "You surely don't mean to suggest . . ."

"I do," Jason said, eyes blazing. "Ulysses Moore is still with us. Somehow, some way, he's guiding us, leading us along on this incredible journey."

"You'll have to forgive Jason," Julia said to Nestor. "When it comes to ghosts and freaky weird stuff, he's a total believer."

"If you've got another explanation, Julia, I'm all ears," Jason retorted. "But regardless, the fact is that we've failed totally. We found the map, but Oblivia took it away. Manfred stole the key. They destroyed the House of Mirrors. They win every battle. And we," he said, "fail at every turn."

Nestor pulled himself to full height. He made a decision. "From this moment forward," he said, his voice deadly serious, "you will do exactly as I say."

The kids looked at him, shocked.

"What?!"

"You have not failed," Nestor said, spitting out the words. "Don't think that way, not for a moment."

He paused, unable to find the right words. "Come," he said. "I have something to show you."

Nestor marched down the hallway with Jason, Rick, and Julia at his heels. He stopped suddenly, cupped his hands, and said to Jason, "Up you go."

"Um, excuse me?" Jason said. He looked at the ceiling. There was nothing there.

"It is well concealed," Nestor said. "But look harder. You may see two hairline cracks running parallel. And there," he pointed to the ceiling, "a little brass ring, painted white."

Jason squinted. "If you say so," he said, and stepped into Nestor's hands.

The old man was surprisingly strong. Rick and Julia steadied Jason by holding his legs. "Okay, I think this is it," Jason murmured. He groped with his fingers. "Yep." He pulled hard. The trapdoor opened slightly.

"Good," Nestor said. "Pull it all the way down, Jason."

The ceiling door folded down, revealing a ladder that expanded until it reached the floor. "A secret attic!" Julia exclaimed. "Very cool, Nestor."

Nestor just smiled mysteriously. "Up you go."

Manfred spent most of the afternoon observing the men from Cyclops. It was pleasant to lounge around watching other people work. And work they did — banging, ripping, shredding, hauling. They moved in and out of the house like ants at a picnic, increasingly covered with dust and debris.

The crane, its iron ball still lodged in the retaining wall, lay on its side. It had been badly damaged. The workmen had finally been able to stop the rotation of the house by destroying the control panel in the basement.

The entire job pained them, nagged at their souls. The men were builders by trade, skilled workers. They admired the House of Mirrors and were awed by the craftsmanship that created it. Unlike Oblivia and Manfred, they took no pleasure in its destruction.

By dusk, only a metal skeleton and a few brick walls remained. The terraces and railings had been pulled down, most of the walls demolished, the floors ripped up in search of . . . the door.

Oblivia constantly referred to two documents. One was Thomas Bowen's map. But it was not as useful as she had hoped. Bowen's map indicated that a door was here, at the house of Peter Dedalus, but it did not show specifically where. The other document, a meticulous blueprint of the house drawn up by Peter Dedalus himself, was accurate to the smallest detail. However, it left no clue as to the where-abouts of the door.

Watching his boss, Manfred remembered how he had found the blueprint in Peter's store. *A shame about the mess*, he thought to himself, sniggering.

A man hurried out of the house. "Ms. Newton!" he cried. "Come take a look. I think we found it!"

Oblivia rushed inside. Manfred followed her.

The men stood beside an old wooden door, still partly obscured by brick. "It was completely cov-ered over," the foreman explained. "It looked like an ordinary brick wall. But then we realized that something was *inside* it."

"My door," Oblivia purred. She reached out and caressed the wood. "My beautiful door."

The workers eyed one another warily. This woman, they had decided, was as nutty as a Snickers bar. She destroyed an entire house . . . just to find a lousy door? It didn't make sense. But a job was a job. It paid good money.

The door had a name carved into it: ULYSSES MOORE. Reading it, Oblivia growled.

The workers stood around uneasily. "Er, ah, Ms. Newton," the foreman spoke up. "Is there anything else you need?"

Oblivia snapped out of her reverie. She took the foreman's face in her hands and, to his shock, kissed him full on the lips. "Yes, yes!" she exclaimed, delighted. "Clear away those last bricks. Free it from this prison!"

The men made short work of it. The door stood fully revealed. "Gee," Manfred mumbled. "It looks exactly like the one at . . . umfff!"

Oblivia had elbowed him sharply in the ribs.

"Quiet, Manfred," she warned in a hiss. "We don't need to share our business with these men."

But of course, Manfred was correct. The door was eerily similar to the one in Cleopatra Biggles' house. This was the magic door, Peter's door. But it was Peter's no more. Now it was Oblivia Newton's door. Her great prize.

Now Oblivia could take the next step. The ultimate prize was that much closer. She instinctively brought her hands to a chain around her neck, where the lion's key hung. Impatiently, Oblivia dismissed the men from the construction crew. "Leave, be gone, your work is done," she told them.

The men looked to their foreman, who shifted on his feet anxiously. "Ms. Newton, er, you said that . . ."

"Ah, payment! In the excitement, I'd forgotten!"

Oblivia said. She pulled out a checkbook, scribbled in it, and handed the foreman a check. He read it, folded it once, and tucked it into his shirt pocket.

"Thank you, Ms. Newton," the foreman said. "That's very generous. We'll just clear this stuff out of the way, pack up our things, and we'll be out of your hair in about an hour or so."

"No," Oblivia retorted. "I want you to leave now, immediately."

"But . . ."

"Come back tomorrow," Oblivia said, sharply.

"Well, er, I guess that's okay," the foreman answered. "We still have to deal with the crane. That's worth a lot of money. We'll need to bring in a winch and . . ."

"Fascinating," Oblivia said with withering sarcasm. "Please tell me all about it . . . another day. I'll pay for the crane in full. As for now, I have things to do. So, ta-ta, gentlemen. Au revoir. Adios. Sayonara."

And so, at last, Oblivia Newton stood before the door she had sought for so long. The lion-shaped key lay in her hand. Her body pulsed with excitement. She still wore a leather motorcycle outfit, but she had brought along a backpack for her travels.

Oblivia slipped the key into the lock. Biting her lip, she turned it.

Clack. The door opened.

Oblivia turned to Manfred. "Take care of things while I'm gone," she instructed. "Don't do anything foolish."

Manfred nodded. "How long do you think it's gonna take?" he wondered.

"I can't say," Oblivia answered. "I must first find Peter on the other side." She smiled. "He will be surprised to see me, I trust."

Oblivia Newton stepped into the darkness, eager to achieve her ultimate triumph.

"Have a nice trip," Manfred grumbled, closing the door behind her. "Don't forget to send me a postcard!"

Manfred looked around, still chuckling over his witty remark. "Send me a postcard," he repeated to himself. "I ought to be a stand-up comic." Manfred scratched his neck and tenderly dabbed at his broken nose. She would be gone for a long time. Days, maybe weeks. No sense hanging around this dump. He was free, free to do whatever he wanted.

And what he wanted most of all was to take a ride. Jump on that motorcycle and put some pavement under his tires. Feel the wind in his hair, take the turns fast and low to the ground, put a hundred miles between him and this place.

He headed for the red motorcycle. It had a full tank of gas and . . . two slashed tires?!

Manfred angrily looked around. He didn't see a soul. Who did this? When?

Manfred howled with rage. He kicked a large rock. Then he howled some more.

The rock, it seemed, had broken his middle toe.

- Chapter 21 -
THE ATTIC

After climbing the ladder, Jason stepped aside from the trapdoor and waited for the others to follow. They found themselves in the dark shadows under Argo Manor's roof. The air was stifling, musty, as if they had climbed into a furnace. With each step, the old boards creaked. They were dry and brittle as old bones.

The attic was covered with a thin layer of dust. Old furniture and boxes had been piled up in various corners. From a couple of dusty, unwashed windows, the pale light of sunset filtered into the room.

Nestor pulled on a string, and a bare bulb lit.

Jason bounced lightly on the floorboards, testing their strength. They groaned under his weight, protesting. The boards reminded Jason of the *Metis*, the ship the kids had sailed to the Land of Punt.

"Stop that," Julia said sharply. Her brother saw that, unlike him, she was uncomfortable, almost frightened.

"Keep moving," Nestor ordered. "Go on."

Julia reached for, and found, her brother's hand. Rick followed just behind the twins. They picked their way through a jumbled path of discarded furniture, trunks, and boxes, and entered an even larger room. It was filled with natural light that came from a dormered window looking down into the courtyard.

Silhouetted against the light, yet still shrouded in shadow, was the shape of a man. He seemed to be waiting for them.

Julia squeezed Jason's hand. Rick protectively reached out, placing himself in front of Julia.

Jason couldn't be sure. He squinted, uncertain. Could it be?

"Mr. Moore?" he whispered, the words barely leaving his throat. He stepped forward.

The man did not answer.

By the window, there was a long wooden table covered with canvases, paints, sketches.

"Mr. Moore?" Jason said again, closing the gap.

There was a loud, sharp noise. The kids whirled to see Nestor, smiling mischievously. He clapped his hands, revealing the source of the sound.

"He can't answer you, Jason," Nestor said with some amusement. "He's just an old stiff." He limped forward, past Jason, and gestured for the kids to follow.

The man who stood beside the drawing table was only a mannequin, an artist's dummy.

Julia punched Nestor on the back of the shoulder. "That's for scaring me half to death," she said.

Everyone laughed, relieving the tension.

"You have to admit," Rick said, "it was kind of funny." He made a frightened face, and slowly stepped toward the mannequin. "Mr. Moore . . . ?" he whimpered. "Mr. Moore? Is that you? It's me, Jason!"

Julia and Nestor roared with laughter.

Jason, oddly, didn't find it all that funny. After all, he thought he'd seen a ghost.

"This was Penelope's little retreat," explained Nestor, standing near the working table. "Her art studio, in fact. This is the room where she painted."

He pointed to stacks of canvases piled high or leaning against the wall. A faint smell of turpentine lingered in the air.

"I have not touched a thing. It is the same as when she . . . left," Nestor confessed. "Her watercolors, her charcoal pencils, the paints — and, of course, Penelope's silent model, Charles." Nestor smiled. "This was Penelope's special place, her home away from home."

"Okaaay," Julia said. "But this is a huge house, Nestor. Why did she work all the way up here?"

Nestor shrugged. "She found it one day and, well, I think she just felt at home here. She had the soul of an artist. Maybe she needed to be at the highest point in the house in order to fly."

Rick walked to the corner of the table. A few chess pieces lay there. They matched those from Peter Dedalus' chessboard.

"Ah, yes, the chess pieces," Nestor commented. "That is one mystery I can help you unravel. It was a grand game they played. They made one move every two weeks, exactly on the second and fourth Monday of every month. For every piece he lost, Peter gave a little invention to Mrs. Moore. And for every piece that she won, Penelope gave Peter one of her paintings."

"Ah," Rick said. "So she would attach the chess piece behind the frame — like she did with the painting at the Bowens'!"

"Evidently so," Nestor agreed.

"Why did you bring us up here?" Jason asked.

Nestor took a deep breath. "Because it is time for you to know," he answered.

"Know?" Jason echoed. "Know what?" He felt the tension building up inside of him, expectant, like a bubble about to burst.

"Time to know who you truly are," Nestor said. He gazed into the faces of Jason, Julia, and Rick, lingering on each one. "Time to know why you are here."

Ulysses Moore no longer had the will, or the energy, to fight," Nestor explained to Jason, Julia, and Rick. "He spent half of his life exploring the doors and investigating their mysteries. The other half he spent trying to protect the secret of this house, the sea inside the cliff, and the ship that awaits, moored at the pier.

"One secret leads to the next, until the secrets pile up, higher and higher. You now possess four keys. They are yours to keep and protect, your secret. But the heart of the mystery is Kilmore Cove itself. This little village by the sea . . ." Nestor's voice trailed off. He seemed to be deep in thought.

"The doors!" he exclaimed at last, pounding a fist into his hand. "The doors of Kilmore Cove take you to places that Ulysses called 'the Ports of Dreams.' Places untouched by the chaos of the modern world. Where there is only peace and beauty. And people who do not need anything more than what they already have. You only need time to rediscover how beautiful it is to swim in the sea, or lie on a beach, or stretch out on the grass to stare at the passing clouds. Time to sit with a book, or to wake at dawn to see the sunrise and try to capture it on canvas. Time to write poetry, to talk with friends, to laugh. Time to discover for yourself that, magically, behind a door, a faraway world awaits you."

The kids stood transfixed, listening with rapt attention. Nestor, who had previously said so little, was now pouring it all out, explaining so much that they were overwhelmed. It was as if a dam inside the old caretaker had burst; all the secrets he had kept bottled up suddenly flowed forth like a torrent.

Nestor continued. "For Ulysses and Penelope, the doors were both magnificent and fearsome, spectacular and treacherous. The Moores knew that if the keys fell into the wrong hands, it would allow all the ills of this world to invade that magical world on the other side. All would be destroyed, like a disease infecting a pure culture."

"Oblivia," Julia said out loud.

Nestor locked eyes with Julia and nodded. "Yes, Oblivia," he confirmed. "She is the danger. She opens the door to greed and sickness, evil and corruption. Ulysses did not want her to poison Kilmore Cove. He wished to preserve it, to protect it, like his ancestors had before him. So he and a small band of friends gathered together. They strived to keep Kilmore Cove far from the dangers of the modern world. But," Nestor said with a heavy sigh, "it was like trying to hold back a rising tide."

Nestor rubbed the back of his neck. His words came softer now, with a trace of sadness. "Of course, one cannot hold back the rising tide. They were doomed to failure, I suppose. Oblivia came to Kilmore Cove."

"And Peter told her the secret," Rick said.

"Yes," Nestor said, "but do not be too hard on poor Peter Dedalus. He failed, yes, but I'm sure he suffered for it a thousand times over. If not Peter, it would have been someone else. We are but human. Imperfect creatures, flawed, weak . . . Anyway, let me continue the story of brave Ulysses," Nestor declared, changing the mood. "Ulysses was mentally and physically drained. Utterly exhausted. He had lost his great love, Penelope. He was abandoned by his friends. He felt alone. Yes, I was still here with him, but it was not enough. Before dying, he hoped that someone else might take up the fight."

Nestor paused, staring at the kids. They were so young, still so pure; they carried in their hearts all the hopes for the future world. They listened, and most important of all, *they believed*.

Nestor smiled and bowed his head ever so slightly. "I believe that his wish has been granted. For you have come to take his place," he said solemnly.

The caretaker of Argo Manor lifted a hat — very gently, very carefully — off the mannequin's head. The hat had a wide brim, with an anchor embroidered in the center of a golden medallion.

"This was his hat," Nestor said. "The hat that he always wore when he became captain of the *Metis* and sailed to distant worlds." Nestor shook it, dispersing the dust. "It belongs on the head of a true captain — on the head of someone who knows the *Metis*, who can lead her to the farthest Port of Dreams. It belongs with you, Jason Covenant," Nestor said. He placed the hat on the boy's head.

Nestor took the jacket off the mannequin. Like a gentleman, he graciously put it around Julia. "And this now belongs to you, Julia Covenant," he declared.

Finally, Nestor unhooked the shoulder strap of a silver sable and handed it to Rick. "And this is for you, Rick Banner," he concluded.

All three kids stood dumbfounded, unable to utter a single word.

The torch had been passed.

"Ulysses assumed that he would surrender his position to one person," Nestor explained. "He prepared this uniform for the time when I found that special person. Yet strangely, and to my great

surprise, I found three. Three special people: Jason, Julia, and Rick.

"I made a sacred vow," the caretaker told them. "I would not divulge all that I knew about Argo Manor and Kilmore Cove until I had found the new protector. Only then could I pass on the secret as it has been handed down for generations to all the previous owners of this house."

Jason's mind reeled. "Do you mean to say that each one of the portraits on the staircase . . ."

". . . was a keeper of the secret," Nestor said with a nod. "Yes, and now you join that sacred tradition. The choice has been made. The rest is up to you, if you wish. If you are willing to accept!"

"Yes! I accept!" Jason said without hesitation.

Nestor looked to the others, Julia and Rick. "All three of you must accept," he said. "Together, or none at all."

Rick spoke first. "I love Kilmore Cove," Rick began. "I have lived here all my life. It's my home. I will always protect it."

Julia hesitated, literally shaking with nervous anxiety. Unlike Jason, who decided so easily — and perhaps a little impulsively — Julia felt a tremendous weight of responsibility on her shoulders. Self-doubt plagued her thoughts. Would she be strong enough? Was she good enough? Could she do it?

"Yes," Julia finally whispered. "Yes, yes, yes. I accept."

Nestor bowed to the children. Then he stood tall, chin lifted, and said, "From this moment forward, I name you Guardians of the Door to Time."

– Chapter 23 –
A NEW BEGINNING

Mrs. Covenant called later that night. The moving company had made a real mess of things, she reported unhappily.

"I'm so frustrated," she confided in Julia. "Part of me just wants to scrap everything and buy all new furniture. It's been one disaster after another."

"Oh, that's too bad," Julia said. "We miss you."

"I miss you, too, Julia," her mother answered. "But at this point, I realize that I simply must stay on top of these men every second of the job. The moment I turn my back, whoops, crash, there goes another mistake."

Julia smiled. In the stone room, Jason and Rick were making plans. For Jason, that meant making things as complicated as possible. Julia stretched the telephone cord to the limit and stuck her head into the room. The boys were huddled on the floor, shoulder to shoulder, staring at a sheet of paper.

"Is Jason behaving?" asked Mrs. Covenant.

"He's actually been . . . not as horrible as usual," Julia said. Coming from her, that was a compliment.

"There's been no trouble?" her mother asked.

"Trouble?!" Julia repeated. "Mom, please. We're stuck here in the middle of nowhere. How could we possibly get into trouble?"

"Oh, sweetheart," Mrs. Covenant replied, "you'll

get used to it over time. I know you miss the fast pace of London, but I think you'll come to like the peace and quiet."

"I guess," Julia said, trying to suppress a laugh.

"We'll be back tomorrow," Mrs. Covenant concluded. "I promise. Don't you worry, sweetums."

"We're okay, Mom. Honest," Julia answered. Sweetums? Yuck! Sometimes her mom made Julia want to hurl.

"Okay, darling?"

"Sure, Mom."

"I'll see you tomorrow evening, then."

"You bet."

"Be good, now. Love you!"

"I love you, too, Mom. For real," Julia said.

After hanging up the phone, Julia rested her head on the back of the chair. She listened to the wind blowing outside the window. Night had come, and she felt very tired. Yawning, she joined the boys.

"So, what did she say?" Jason asked.

"They'll be back tomorrow night," Julia answered.

Rick and Jason exchanged high-fives. "That means we have a little more time!" Jason said happily. "We have so much to do before they get back."

Julia grunted. "I'm fried," she confessed.

Jason looked at Rick; his eyes looked red, weary.

Dinner was almost ready — finally. Soon after, Rick would have to go home. The very thought depressed him.

Julia sat down beside the boys. "So what have you two guys figured out?" she asked. Papers filled with names, colored squares, arrows, and diagrams were scattered on the floor. A typical Jason Covenant creation, insanely complicated and far too confusing. Still, his enthusiasm was infectious.

"First, we have to figure out what Oblivia Newton is going to try to do next," Jason said.

"I think she's going after Peter Dedalus," Rick told Julia.

She nodded in agreement. Oblivia had the key. She found the door. It only made sense.

"Peter led her to believe that he knew a way to control all of the doors," Rick stated. "Oblivia wants that power desperately. I'm sure that she's going to try to find Peter."

"He may be in great danger," Jason said.

"But where will he be?" Julia wondered. "Where does his door go?"

"I guess we could study the notebooks that Ulysses left in the tower," Julia suggested. "Maybe there's a clue in there?"

"One way or the other," Jason said with determination, "we have to find Peter before Oblivia gets to him."

"He knows the secrets," Rick said. "Everything points to him. We're going to have to sail on the *Metis* again . . . and somehow find a man who could be hiding anywhere in the world, at any *time* in the world."

"That's worse than a needle in a haystack," Julia said, her voice gloomy.

"We'll find him," Jason said. He was full of confidence, and the others were grateful to him for it.

And so it came time for Rick to return home. "I'll see you tomorrow," he told Jason and Julia, "in school."

"School?!" Jason groaned. "But we still have so much to learn — we can't go to school tomorrow."

"My brother has a point," Julia said, a sly grin on her face.

"Yes," Rick agreed, laughing. "Too bad it's on the top of his head."

After watching Rick ride his bicycle into the night, Jason found Nestor in the kitchen. He had more questions. He still ached to know more, more, more.

Julia, on the other hand, had reached her limit. Exhausted, she imagined how Ulysses must have felt, fighting the same battle, day after day, year after

year. "I have to sleep," she told Jason and Nestor. On an impulse, she reached for the old man and hugged him. "Thank you," she whispered, "for everything."

"Sleep tight, dear girl," Nestor said gently. "You earned it."

But as she walked up the stairs, drowsy and dazed, Julia thought she heard a voice.

"Did you call me?" she said, looking back toward the kitchen.

No answer, no sound.

She must have been mistaken.

So tired, so ready for sleep.

A gust of wind swept through her hair. A window on the second floor banged loudly; the mirrored door of the tower suddenly slammed shut.

Julia gasped. She grabbed the banister tightly. Instinctively, she reached a hand into her pocket and wrapped her fingers around the four precious keys to the Door to Time.

"Julia!" Jason's voice cried, threading up the stairs. "Please close the tower window! There's a draft down here!"

Julia felt the draft sweeping past her ankles. It was coming from beneath the mirrored door. She walked toward it, nerves jangled, and entered the room. As expected, the same window had mysteriously opened again. A strong breeze poured into the house. Julia closed it firmly, even though she knew it was a lost cause. The window would open again and again as if of its own volition.

She turned to leave, then stopped, paralyzed.

Something had changed. The room was different. She sniffed. There was a smell, familiar yet... unknown. A pungent odor. Julia had smelled it before — somewhere, today perhaps — but she could not remember where.

Fear crawled through her. It was just a feeling, she told herself, there was no reason to be afraid. Barely breathing, she scanned the room. What had changed? What was different?

Then she saw it, and a cold shiver ran up her spine.

In the middle of the desk lay one of Ulysses Moore's journals. Resting on top of it there was a small wooden model of a boat. A gondola, in fact.

Venice, Julia thought.

Jason's unseen hand. Someone was guiding them, helping them, leading them to ... where?

Julia set the gondola aside. She opened the journal. It contained notes written by Ulysses Moore. The notes were about a journey to Venice.

On the first page, there was a sketch of the lion statue in Saint Mark's Square.

The lion's key! Julia thought. *Peter.*

She raced out of the room, down the stairs, and into the kitchen. Heart pounding, she skidded in stocking feet in front of Jason and Nestor, who had been snacking at the kitchen table.

"What happened?" Jason asked, immediately recognizing that something was up.

Julia stared about wildly, almost incoherent. She threw open the front door and stepped out into the courtyard. She clutched the journal in her hand, turning, turning all around in the dark. "Where are you?" she screamed into the night. Her eyes searched the trees and garden. "Where are you hiding?!"

Branches swayed in the sea breeze. An owl hooted, then another. Far below, the surf pounded against the rocks of Salton Cliff. The rest was silence — silence and nothingness.

No one was outside.

"Julia?" Jason came to his sister and took her hand. "What is it? What's happened?"

She again searched the shadows of the garden, the roof, the windows, and the long gnarled branches of the sycamores. She searched — and finally surrendered to the magic.

MORE PEOPLE FROM KILMORE COVE

Miss. Calypso

Leonard Minaxo

Gwendaline Mainoff

Mrs. and Mr. Bowen

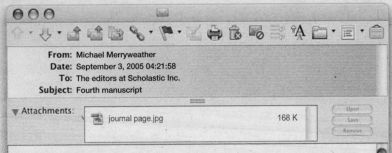

From: Michael Merryweather
Date: September 3, 2005 04:21:58
To: The editors at Scholastic Inc.
Subject: Fourth manuscript

Attachments: journal page.jpg — 168 K

I'm still in Cornwall. After deciphering Ulysses Moore's third journal, I quickly set to work with the fourth. I just translated a very interesting piece, and I'm sending it to you because I know that like me, you're probably dying to know what happened next.

Peter Dedalus was alive! Of this Rick, Jason, and Julia were certain. They were also sure that the shadow of Saint Mark's lion would lead him to his laboratory. But first they had to find the Black Gondolier, the only person who could track the city's canals back to the Island of the Masks. If they wanted to find Peter's refuge, they needed to do it in a hurry.

"In all probability, Oblivia will get there before us," Julia worried.

"Don't even think that, little sister," Jason warned her.

"Listen guys, I've got an idea," Rick whispered, looking around him.

As soon as I find out anything else, I'll let you know.

MM

PS: The attached is one of the drawings I found in Ulysses' fourth journal.

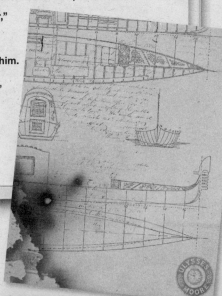

ULYSSES MOORE #4:
THE ISLAND OF MASKS
COMING MAY 2008